AMERICAN SCHOOL TEXTBOOK
VOCABULARY KEY

GRADE 1

Michael A. Putlack

FUN學 美國英語課本

各學科關鍵英單 二版＋Workbook

MP3
寂天雲 APP

如何下載 MP3 音檔

❶ 寂天雲 APP 聆聽：掃描書上 QR Code 下載「寂天雲－英日語學習隨身聽」APP。加入會員後，用 APP 內建掃描器再次掃描書上 QR Code，即可使用 APP 聆聽音檔。

❷ 官網下載音檔：請上「寂天閱讀網」（www.icosmos.com.tw），註冊會員／登入後，搜尋本書，進入本書頁面，點選「MP3 下載」下載音檔，存於電腦等其他播放器聆聽使用。

FÜN學美國英語課本

各學科關鍵英單 GRADE 1

AMERICAN SCHOOL TEXTBOOK
VOCABULARY KEY

二版

作者簡介

Michael A. Putlack

專攻歷史與英文，擁有美國麻州 Tufts University 碩士學位。

作　　　者　Michael A. Putlack

　　　　　　Zachany Fillinghan / Shara Dupuis（Workbook B 大題）

編　　　輯　丁宥暄／李盈瑩

翻　　　譯　李盈瑩

校　　　對　歐寶妮

封面設計　林書玉

內頁排版　林書玉

製程管理　洪巧玲

發 行 人　黃朝萍

出 版 者　寂天文化事業股份有限公司

電　　　話　+886-(0)2-2365-9739

傳　　　真　+886-(0)2-2365-9835

網　　　址　www.icosmos.com.tw

讀者服務　onlineservice@icosmos.com.tw

出版日期　2023 年 7 月　二版二刷　（寂天雲隨身聽 APP 版）

郵 撥 帳 號　1998620-0 寂天文化事業股份有限公司
訂書金額未滿 1000 元，請外加運費 100 元。
〔若有破損，請寄回更換，謝謝。〕

國家圖書館出版品預行編目資料

FUN 學美國英語課本 Grade 1：各學科關鍵英單 (寂天隨身聽 APP 版) /
Michael A. Putlack 作 . -- 二版 . -- [臺北市]：寂天文化, 2023.07
　面；　公分

ISBN 978-626-300-200-5 (菊 8K 平裝)

1.CST: 英語 2.CST: 詞彙
805.12　　　　　　　　　　　　　　　112010311

FUN學美國英語課本：各學科關鍵英單

進入明星學校必備的英文單字

用美國教科書學英文是最道地的學習方式，有越來越多的學校選擇以美國教科書作為教材，用全英語授課（immersion）的方式教學，讓學生把英語當成母語學習。在一些語言學校裡，也掀起了一波「用美國教科書學英文」的風潮。另外，還有越來越多的父母優先考慮讓子女用美國教科書來學習英文，讓孩子將來能夠進入明星學校或國際學校就讀。

為什麼要使用美國教科書呢？TOEFL 等國際英語能力測驗都是以各學科知識為基礎，使用美國教科書不但能大幅提升英文能力，也可以增加數學、社會、科學等方面的知識，因此非常適合用來準備考試。即使不到國外留學，也可以像在美國上課一樣，而這也是使用美國教科書最吸引人的地方。

以多樣化的照片、插圖和例句來熟悉跨科學習中的英文單字

到底該使用何種美國教科書呢？還有如何才能讀懂美國教科書呢？美國各州、各學校的課程都不盡相同，而學生也有選擇教科書的權利，所以單單是教科書的種類就多達數十種。若不小心選擇到程度不適合的教科書，就很容易造成孩子對學英語的興趣大減。

因此，正確的作法應該要先累積字彙和相關知識背景。我國學生的學習能力很強，只需要培養對不熟悉的用語和跨科學習（Cross-Curricular Study）的適應能力。

本系列網羅了在以全英語教授社會、科學、數學、語言、藝術、音樂等學科時，所有會出現的必備英文單字。只要搭配書中真實的照片、插圖和例句，就能夠把這些在美國小學課本中會出現的各學科核心單字記起來，同時還可以熟悉相關的背景知識。

四種使用頻率最高的美國教科書的字彙分析

本系列套書規畫了 6 個階段的字彙學習課程，搜羅了 McGraw Hill、Harcourt、Pearson 和 Core Knowledge 等四大教科書中的主要字彙，並且整理出各科目、各主題的核心單字，然後依照學年分為 Grade 1 到 Grade 6。

本套書的適讀對象為「準備大學學測指考的學生」和「準備參加 TOEFL 等國際英語能力測驗的學生」。對於「準備赴美唸高中的學生」和「想要看懂美國教科書的學生」，本套書亦是最佳的先修教材。

《FUN學美國英語課本：各學科關鍵英單》系列的結構與特色

1. 本套書中所收錄的英文單字都是美國學生在上課時會學到的字彙和用法。

2. 將美國小學教科書中會出現的各學科核心單字，搭配多樣化照片、插圖和例句，讓讀者更容易熟記。

3. 藉由閱讀教科書式的題目，來強化讀、聽、寫的能力。透過各式各樣的練習與題目，不僅能夠全盤吸收與各主題有關的字彙，也能夠熟悉相關的知識背景。

4. 每一冊的教學大綱（syllabus）皆涵蓋了社會、歷史、地理、科學、數學、語言、美術和音樂等學科，以循序漸進的方式，學習從基礎到高級的各科核心字彙，不僅能夠擴增各科目的字彙量，同時還提升了運用句子的能力。（教學大綱請參考第 8 頁）

5. 可學到社會、科學等的相關背景知識和用語，也有助於準備 TOEFL 等國際英語能力測驗。

6. 對於「英語程度有限，但想看懂美國教科書的學生」來說，本套書是很好的先修教材。

7. 全系列 6 階段共分為 6 冊，可依照個人英語程度，選擇合適的分冊。

   Grade 1 美國小學 1 年級課程　　**Grade 2** 美國小學 2 年級課程

   Grade 3 美國小學 3 年級課程　　**Grade 4** 美國小學 4 年級課程

   Grade 5 美國小學 5 年級課程　　**Grade 6** 美國小學 6 年級課程

8. 書末附有關鍵字彙的中英文索引，方便讀者搜尋與查照（請參考第 141 頁）。

強烈建議下列學生使用本套書：

1. 「準備大學學測指考」的學生

2. 「準備參加以全英語授課的課程，想熟悉美國學生上課時會用到的各科核心字彙」的學生

3. 「對美國小學各科必備英文字彙已相當熟悉，想朝高級單字邁進」美國學校的七年級生

4. 「準備赴美唸高中」的學生

MP3

收錄了本書的「Key Words」、「Power Verbs」、「Word Families」單元中的所有單字和例句，和「Checkup」中 E 大題的文章，以及 Workbook 中 A 大題聽寫練習文章。

AMERICAN SCHOOL TEXTBOOK

VOCABULARY KEY

Workbook

GRADE 1

Michael A. Putlack

FUN學美國英語課本

各學科關鍵英單 二版

Unit 01

Listen to the passage and fill in the blanks.

🎧 121   **Good Neighbors**

Your 1._____ are the people who live near you. In our 2._____, people help each other and 3._____ one another. If you want to have a good neighbor, you have to be a good neighbor first. There are many ways to do this. First, you can be nice to your neighbors. Always 4._____ them and say, "Hello." 5._____ them. Become friends with them. Also, don't be noisy at your home. And 6._____ your neighbors' 7._____. If they have any problems, help them out. They will help you too in the future. If you do all of these things, you can be a good neighbor.

B **Read the passage above and answer the following questions.**

_____ 8. Another good title for this passage would be _____.
- a How to Be a Good Neighbor
- b How to Find Good Neighbors
- c Why Neighbors Are Important
- d Why Neighborhood Safety Is Important

_____ 9. Which of the following advice does the passage provide?
- a Ignore your neighbors.
- b Always agree with your neighbors.
- c Try to be quiet in your house.
- d Dress in the same clothes as your neighbors.

_____ 10. "If they have any problem, help them out." Which of the following has the same meaning as the word "problem"?
- a Solution.
- b Difficulty.
- c Neighbor.
- d Success.

Unit 02

A Listen to the passage and fill in the blanks.

🎧 122 | **A Day at School**

John and Sally go to 1._____ school. Their first 2._____ starts at 8 a.m. They go to their 3._____. They stand up, face the flag, and say the 4._____ of 5._____ before their class begins. Then their teacher, Mrs. Smith, starts their lessons. They study math, social studies, English, and art, and then they go to the 6._____ for lunch. After lunch, they have 7._____, so all the students go outside and play for a while. Then they learn science, history, and music. Finally, it's 3 o'clock. It's time for them to go home!

B Read the passage above and answer the following questions.

_____ 8. What's the purpose of this passage?
    [a] To teach good study skills.
    [b] To compare schools in different countries.
    [c] To describe a regular day for John and Sally.
    [d] To show how John and Sally met.

_____ 9. "Their first class stars at 8 a.m." Which of the following has the opposite meaning to the word "first"?
    [a] Before.
    [b] Last.
    [c] Middle.
    [d] Beginning.

_____ 10. Which of the following is a subject that John and Sally do NOT study in school?
    [a] English.
    [b] Art.
    [c] Drama.
    [d] Music.

A Listen to the passage and fill in the blanks.

🎧 123 **Different Customs and Cultures**

Americans have their own 1._____ and 2._____. But many other countries have these, too. We should know about other people's customs and cultures. And we should always 3._____ them. For example, in America, people wear their shoes in their homes. But in some 4._____ countries like Japan and Korea, people 5. _____ their shoes before going inside their homes. And Americans eat with 6._____ and 7._____. But in India and other countries, people often eat with their hands. There are many other differences. And we should know and learn about them.

B Read the passage above and answer the following questions.

_____ 8. "But all of these cultures are special." A word that has a similar meaning to "special" is _____.
  a strange
  b important
  c religious
  d unique

_____ 9. Which of the following statements is true?
  a Poor people eat with their hands.
  b Rich countries have forks and knives.
  c People eat food in different ways.
  d We should all learn to use chopsticks.

_____ 10. People's customs and cultures should be _____.
  a respected
  b ignored
  c followed
  d obeyed

Unit 04

Listen to the passage and fill in the blanks.

🎧 124 **The Leaders of the American Government**

The 1._____ is the leader of the American 2._____. He is 3._____ by the people and serves for four years. He lives in the White House. There are other government 4._____, too. Many serve in Congress. Congress is divided into two parts. They are the Senate and the House of Representatives. Every state has two 5._____. And every state has a different number of 6._____ in the House. Some have many. But some have just one or two. The members of Congress make all the 7._____ for the country. They work from the Capitol in Washington, D.C.

Read the passage above and answer the following questions.

_____ 8. Who is the leader of the American government?
- a Congress.
- b The president.
- c The Capitol.
- d The Senate.

_____ 9. The article says the president is "elected" by the people. Another way of saying "elected" is _____.
- a hated
- b known
- c ignored
- d chosen

_____ 10. This article is mostly about a _____.
- a government
- b country
- c law
- d city

Unit 05

A Listen to the passage and fill in the blanks.

🎧 125 **Christian Holidays**

Christians are people who believe in 1._____. They believe that Jesus Christ is the son of God. In Christianity, there are two very important 2._____. They are 3._____ and 4._____. Christmas is on December 25. Christians 5._____ the birth of Jesus on this day. Christmas is a time of happiness and celebration. Easter is in late March or early April every year. It is the most important Christian holiday. It is the day when Jesus Christ came back from the 6._____. Most Christians go to 7._____ on this day.

B Read the passage above and answer the following questions.

_____ 8. "Christmas is a time of happiness and celebration." The word "celebration" means a(n)_____.
- a special tool
- b party
- c animal
- d religion

_____ 9. According to the article, which of the following statements is true?
- a Christians celebrate Easter in December.
- b Christmas is when Jesus came back to life.
- c Christmas and Easter are Christian holidays.
- d Most Christians stay away from church on Easter.

_____ 10. This passage is about _____.
- a important people in history
- b churches
- c gifts
- d religious holidays

Unit 06

A **Listen to the passage and fill in the blanks.**

🎧 126 | **National Parks**

The United States has many national parks. These are 1._____ areas. So people cannot develop or 2._____ them.

The first national park was Yellowstone National Park. It is an area with 3._____ 4._____ and many wild animals. The Grand Canyon is also a national park. It is one of the largest 5._____ in the world. Every year, millions of people visit these parks. They tour the parks and go 6._____. Some even camp in the parks. They learn about the land and how to 7._____ it, too.

B **Read the passage above and answer the following questions.**

_____ 8. What is the main idea of this passage?
- a The United States was the first country to have national parks.
- b There are several protected nature areas in the United States.
- c How beautiful the Yellowstone National Park is.
- d Why the Grand Canyon is not a national park.

_____ 9. Which of the following is the opposite of a "wild" animal?
- a A pet.
- b A tiger.
- c A wolf.
- d A bear.

_____ 10. The article says Yellowstone National Park has "stunning" scenery. The word "stunning" means _____.
- a very beautiful
- b not clear
- c very tall
- d hard to miss

7

Unit 07

A Listen to the passage and fill in the blanks.

🎧 127 **Oceans and Continents**

There are seven 1._____ on Earth. 2._____ is the biggest of all of them. 3._____ has many countries located in it. 4._____ has both deserts and jungles in it. Asia, Europe, and Africa are often called "the Old World." 5._____ is the largest island on Earth. People call North and South America "the New World."

There are five oceans on Earth. The 6._____ is the biggest. The 7._____ lies between the Old World and the New World. The 8._____ Ocean is the only ocean named for a country. The Arctic and Antarctic oceans are both very cold.

B Read the passage above and answer the following questions.

_____ 9. Which of the following oceans is very cold?
　　　a The Atlantic Ocean
　　　b The Arctic Ocean.
　　　c The Indian Ocean.
　　　d The Pacific Ocean.

_____ 10. Another good title for this article would be _____.
　　　a A Description of Earth
　　　b The Birth of Earth
　　　c The Continents of Earth
　　　d The Oceans of Earth

_____ 11. "Europe has many countries located in it." Which of the following words means the same as "located"?
　　　a Moved.
　　　b Settled.
　　　c Passed.
　　　d Called.

Unit 08

Listen to the passage and fill in the blanks.

🎧 128 | **What Is a Map?**

1._____ are 2._____ of different places. They show what an area looks like. Some maps show very large areas, like countries. Other maps show small areas, like cities or 3._____.

Maps can show many things. On big maps, they show the land and water. These maps have countries, seas, oceans, and even 4._____ on them. People use these maps to find 5._____ and cities. Small maps might show one city or area. They have many 6._____. They have 7._____ buildings and streets on them. People use these maps to find their way somewhere.

B **Read the passage above and answer the following questions.**

_____ 8. "Maps are drawings of different places." Another word for "drawings" is _____.
- a information
- b pictures
- c facts
- d samples

_____ 9. This article is about _____.
- a a tool to find places
- b a part of the world
- c a certain city
- d a very old book

_____ 10. What will you NOT find on a big map?
- a An individual building.
- b A continent.
- c An ocean.
- d A country.

Unit 09

A Listen to the passage and fill in the blanks.

🎧 129

Endangered Animals

There are many animals on the Earth. Some 1._____ have many animals. But there are just a few animals in other species. These animals are 2._____. If we aren't careful, they could all 3._____ and become 4._____. In China, the panda is endangered. In the oceans, the blue whale is endangered. In Africa, lions, tigers, and elephants are all endangered. There are many other endangered animals, too. What can people do? People can stop 5._____ them. And people can 6._____ land for the animals to 7._____. Then, maybe one day, they will not be endangered anymore.

B Read the passage above and answer the following questions.

_____ 8. What is the main idea of the article?
- a We can save endangered animals.
- b There is a panda emergency in China.
- c The blue whale is in trouble.
- d There are many different species of panda.

_____ 9. Which of the following is NOT an endangered animal in Africa?
- a Lions.
- b Pandas.
- c Tigers.
- d Elephants.

_____ 10. "And people can set aside land for the animals to live on." The phrase "set aside" means _____.
- a to start
- b to take away
- c to be side by side with
- d to reserve for a purpose

Unit 10

A Listen to the passage and fill in the blanks.

🎧 130 | **The Spanish in the New World**

Christopher Columbus discovered the 1._____ in 1492. After him, many Europeans began to visit the land. Most of the early 2._____ came from Spain. The Spanish wanted to get rich. So they looked for gold and silver. They were often very 3._____ to the natives.

They made 4._____ on them. So the Spanish killed many 5._____. They 6._____ the Aztecs. And they also defeated the Incas. They made many natives their 7._____. They were not interested in being friends with them. They just wanted 8._____.

B Read the passage above and answer the following questions.

_____ 9. What is this article's purpose?
- a To describe the fall of the Spanish Empire.
- b To describe the Spanish colonization of the Americas.
- c To describe the fall of the Aztecs and Incas.
- d To describe Inca and Aztec culture.

_____ 10. Another good title for this article might be _____.
- a When Spain Came to the Americas
- b The Fall of the Aztecs
- c The Invention of Cannons
- d The Last Days of the Inca Emperor

_____ 11. "The Spanish were very cruel to the natives." The word "cruel" means _____.
- a mean
- b cool
- c angry
- d fair

Unit 11

Listen to the passage and fill in the blanks.

🎧 131   **Seasons and Weather**

There are four 1.＿＿＿＿＿＿＿ in a year. They are 2.＿＿＿＿＿＿＿, summer,

3.＿＿＿＿＿＿, and 4.＿＿＿＿＿＿. Sometimes people say "5.＿＿＿＿＿＿" instead

of fall. Each season has different kinds of 6.＿＿＿＿＿＿＿. In spring, the air

gets warmer, and the weather is often 7.＿＿＿＿＿＿. Everything comes back

to life. Flowers start to 8.＿＿＿＿＿＿＿, and leaves start growing on trees.

In summer, the weather is usually very hot and 9.＿＿＿＿＿＿＿. In fall, the

10.＿＿＿＿＿＿＿ starts to decrease. The weather gets cooler. The leaves

on trees start changing colors. Winter is the coldest season. It usually

11.＿＿＿＿＿＿ during the winter.

B Read the passage above and answer the following questions.

＿＿＿＿＿ 12. Which statement best expresses the main idea of this article?

     a A year is divided into four seasons.

     b Summer is always warmer than winter.

     c Flowers begin to bloom in spring.

     d Some seasons are longer than others.

＿＿＿＿＿ 13. This article focuses on ＿＿＿＿＿.

     a the planet

     b seasons

     c autumn

     d snow

＿＿＿＿＿ 14. "In fall, the temperature starts to decrease." The word "decrease" means ＿＿＿＿＿.

     a to stay the same

     b to become uncomfortable

     c to go down

     d to become cold

Unit 12

A Listen to the passage and fill in the blanks.

🎧 132 | **How Plants Grow**

> Let's grow some 1._____ in a garden. First, we need some seeds. We have to plant the seeds in the 2._____, and then we should give them water. After a few days or weeks, the plants will start growing above the ground. First, they will be tiny, but they will become taller every day.
>
> Now, the plants need plenty of 3._____, water, and 4._____ in order to get bigger. Slowly, the 5._____ will grow higher, and the plants will get branches and 6._____. Some of them will start to 7._____. These blossoms will turn into fruit we can eat later. A part of these blossoms makes seeds. They help plants make new plants.

B Read the passage above and answer the following questions.

_____ 8. Which sentence best expresses the main idea of the article?
  a Growing plants in a garden is very difficult.
  b It's a very good idea to grow your plants inside the house.
  c Plants in a garden need several things to grow.
  d A beautiful garden will have many different types of plants.

_____ 9. Which of the following is NOT something that plants need in order to grow?
  a Sunlight.
  b Wind.
  c Nutrients.
  d Water.

_____ 10. "These blossoms will turn into fruit we can eat later." The word "blossom" in this sentence is referring to _____.
  a a part of a plant
  b a type of seed
  c a type of soil
  d a gardening tool

A **Listen to the passage and fill in the blanks.**

🎧 133 **Places to Live**

An animal's 1._____ is very important. It has everything an animal needs to 2._____. Most animals can't 3._____ other habitats. Fish live in the water. They can't survive in the 4._____. Deer live in the 5._____. They can't survive in the jungle.

What makes a habitat 6._____? There are many things. Two of them are more important than the others. They are weather and 7._____. These two help certain plants grow. Many animals use these plants for food and 8._____. Without them, the animals could not live in those habitats.

B **Read the passage above and answer the following questions.**

_____ 9. What is closest to the main point of the article that the author wants to make?
- a Habitats are often hard to find.
- b Habitats are very complicated.
- c Habitats are very important.
- d Habitats are increasing in number.

_____ 10. Which of the following statements is true?
- a An animal's habitat changes very often.
- b An animal's habitat provides food and shelter.
- c Not all animals have a habitat.
- d The most important thing about a habitat is its appearance.

_____ 11. "An animal's habitat is very important." The word "habitat" means _____.
- a the location in which an animal lives
- b the types of food an animal eats
- c the temperature that best suits the animal
- d an animal's defense against diseases

A Listen to the passage and fill in the blanks.

🎧 134 | **Fishing and Overfishing**

The 1._____ has many different habitats for many plants and animals. It helps the Earth stay healthy. So we have to be careful not to hurt the ocean. Many people around the world enjoy eating 2._____. Fishermen catch food in the ocean for us to eat. This includes 3._____ as well as fish. Shellfish are animals like 4._____, 5._____, 6._____, and 7._____. Because people eat so much seafood, there are many 8._____. Unfortunately, the fishermen are catching too many fish these days. So the number of fish in the oceans is decreasing. Many fishing 9._____ are getting smaller and smaller. Fishermen need to stop catching so many fish. They must give the fish time to increase their numbers.

B Read the passage above and answer the following questions.

_____ 10. What is closest to the main point the author wants to make in the article?
   a Humans have mastered the art of fishing.
   b A diet based on seafood is very healthy.
   c Humans are fishing too much.
   d New types of seafood are discovered every day.

_____ 11. This article is about a(n) _____.
   a industry   b type of fish
   c diet   d region

_____ 12. "They must give the fish time to increase their numbers." What does the word "their" refer to?
   a Time.
   b Fish.
   c The ocean.
   d Fishermen.

A Listen to the passage and fill in the blanks.

🎧 135 **Staying Healthy**

A person's body is like a 1._____. It has many parts that help keep it running. If these parts are running well, a person will be healthy. But sometimes a person's body 2._____. Then that person gets sick.

Many times, 3._____ make a person sick. When germs 4._____ a body, it needs to fight back. Sometimes, the person's body alone can 5._____ the germs. Other times, the person might need 6._____ from a doctor to get better. Fortunately, many medicines can kill germs and help bodies become healthy again.

B Read the passage above and answer the following questions.

_____ 7. Which statement best expresses the main idea of this article?
- a Sometimes people get sick.
- b Sickness is like a machine.
- c Always see a doctor for medicine.
- d It's difficult to break a machine.

_____ 8. This article focuses on _____.
- a medicine for colds
- b doctors
- c the human body
- d machines

_____ 9. People often get sick because of _____.
- a medicine
- b diet
- c exercise
- d germs

Listen to the passage and fill in the blanks.

🎧 136 | **How Can Water Change?**

Water has three forms. It can be a 1._____, a 2._____, or a 3._____. Why does it change? It changes because of the temperature. Water's normal state is liquid. But water sometimes becomes a solid. Why? It gets too cold. Water freezes when 4._____ is taken away from it. Water in its solid form is called 5._____. Also, sometimes water becomes a gas. Why? It gets too hot. Water 6._____ when its temperature gets high enough. Then it turns into 7._____. This steam is a gas. When water is a gas, it is called water 8._____.

B **Read the passage above and answer the following questions.**

_____ 9. Which statement best expresses the main idea of this article?
     a Water is very plentiful on Earth.
     b Water can be a liquid, gas, or solid.
     c Water turns to gas when heated.
     d Water turns to ice when cooled.

_____ 10. Which of the following is NOT one of water's forms?
     a Cold.
     b Liquid.
     c Gas.
     d Solid.

_____ 11. "Water boils when its temperature gets high enough." The word "temperature" means _____.
     a the type of container something goes in
     b how hot or cold something is
     c a change of forms something goes through
     d how well something flows

A **Listen to the passage and fill in the blanks.**

🎧 137 | **Measuring Food** |

It's time to make some cookies. We have all of the 1._____. Now, we need to 2._____ everything before we start cooking.

First, we need 1 cup of butter. After that, we need $\frac{3}{4}$ cup of white sugar, the same amount of brown sugar, and $2\frac{1}{4}$ cups of 3._____. We also need $1\frac{1}{2}$ 4._____ of vanilla 5._____, 1 teaspoon of baking 6._____, and $\frac{1}{2}$ teaspoon of salt. We have to measure $1\frac{1}{2}$ cups of chocolate 7._____, too. Finally, we need 2 eggs. Now we have measured all of our ingredients. Let's start cooking.

B **Read the passage above and answer the following questions.**

_____ 8. Which statement best expresses the main idea of this article?
- a You have to measure ingredients when making cookies.
- b Different countries have different measurements.
- c The best cooks measure by eye alone.
- d Brown sugar is a key ingredient when baking.

_____ 9. "We have all of the ingredients." Which of the following is closest in meaning to the word "ingredient?"
- a A type of cookie.
- b A part of a mixture.
- c A measuring cup.
- d An oven.

_____ 10. "Now we have measured all of our ingredients." The word with a similar meaning to "measured" is _____.
- a weighed
- b divided
- c eaten
- d purchased

Unit 18

A Listen to the passage and fill in the blanks.

🎧 138 **Benjamin Franklin**

Benjamin Franklin was a great American 1._____. He lived more than 200 years ago. He was very curious about 2._____. He thought that it was 3._____. But he wasn't sure. So he decided to do an 4._____.

Franklin tied a metal key to a 5._____. Then he waited for a storm to begin. He 6._____ the kite in the storm. Lightning was 7._____ in the area. Electric 8._____ from the lightning got on the key. When Franklin touched the key, he got shocked. He had just proved that lightning was a form of 9._____!

B Read the passage above and answer the following questions.

_____ 10. Which sentence best expresses the main idea of this article?
  a Benjamin Franklin was an American.
  b Benjamin Franklin enjoyed watching lightning storms.
  c Benjamin Franklin tied a key to the end of a kite string.
  d Benjamin Franklin proved that lightning was electricity.

_____ 11. What proved to Benjamin Franklin that lightning was electricity?
  a He wore a metal hat and was struck by lightning.
  b He touched his kite key and received a shock.
  c His kite was struck by lightning and burned up.
  d He observed lightning for several years.

_____ 12. "He was very curious about lightning." If a person is "curious" about something, he _____.
  a is scared of it
  b knows everything about it
  c wants to know more about it
  d has never seen it

19

Listen to the passage and fill in the blanks.

139 **Is Pluto a Planet?**

The 1._____ system is the sun and the 2._____ going around the sun. There are eight planets in it. In order of distance from the sun, they are: Mercury, 3._____, Earth, 4._____ , Jupiter, Saturn, Uranus, and Neptune. Scientists used to consider 5._____ the ninth planet in the solar system. But they do not think that way now. Instead, they consider Pluto to be a minor planet. There are many 6._____ like Pluto in the 7._____ solar system. And scientists don't think they are planets. So they don't consider Pluto a planet anymore.

B **Read the passage above and answer the following questions.**

_____ 8. Which sentence best expresses the main idea of this article?
　　　 a Pluto is the most important planet in the solar system.
　　　 b Pluto is no longer considered to be a planet.
　　　 c Scientists have discovered several planets just like Pluto.
　　　 d Pluto is believed to have many valuable resources on it.

_____ 9. Which of the following is a reason why Pluto is no longer a planet?
　　　 a Its name made some people angry.
　　　 b There were already too many planets in the solar system.
　　　 c It was too cold to support life.
　　　 d There were many objects similar to it that aren't planets.

_____ 10. "Instead, they consider Pluto to be a minor planet." The word with the opposite meaning of "minor" is _____.
　　　 a invisible
　　　 b mysterious
　　　 c major
　　　 d regular

Unit 20

A Listen to the passage and fill in the blanks.

🎧 140 **The Layers of the Earth**

The Earth is a huge planet. But it is divided into three parts. They are the 1._____, 2._____, and 3._____. Each section is different from the others.

The crust is the outermost part of the Earth. That's the 4._____ of the Earth. Everything on top of the Earth—the oceans, seas, rivers, mountains, 5._____, and forests —is part of the crust. Beneath the crust, there is a thick 6._____ of hot, 7._____ rock. It's called the mantle. The mantle is the biggest section. The mantle is extremely hot. The innermost part of the Earth is the core. Part of it is solid, and part is 8._____.

B Read the passage above and answer the following questions.

_____ 9. This article is about the Earth's _____.
- a history
- b wildlife
- c sections
- d deserts

_____ 10. Which of the following is NOT true about the Earth's mantle?
- a It is made up of melted rock.
- b It is between the crust and the core.
- c It is extremely hot.
- d It has oceans and rivers.

_____ 11. "The crust is the outermost part of the Earth." Which of the following is the opposite of "outermost"?
- a Top.
- b Surface.
- c Part.
- d Innermost.

Unit 21

A Listen to the passage and fill in the blanks.

 141

Five Simple Shapes

There are five basic 1._____: the 2._____, rectangle, triangle, circle, and oval. There are many other shapes, but they all 3._____ these five basic ones.

Every object has a certain shape. For example, a box may look like a square or 4._____. So does a cube.

A piece of pizza might resemble a 5._____. A soccer ball and a baseball are both 6._____. And eggs are 7._____-shaped. There are also other more complicated shapes. A mountain might resemble a 8._____. And a funnel looks like a cone.

B Read the passage above and answer the following questions.

_____ 9. Which statement below best expresses the main idea of this article?

     a Everything is made up of five basic materials.

     b The triangle is the most complicated shape.

     c Most things look like one of five basic shapes.

     d Two squares can combine into a rectangle.

_____ 10. A baseball is shaped like a(n) _____.

     a square

     b rectangle

     c circle

     d oval

_____ 11. "There are many other shapes, but they all resemble these five basic ones." The word with the opposite meaning of "basic" is _____.

     a round

     b large

     c simple

     d complex

Unit 22

A Listen to the passage and fill in the blanks.

 142

Greater and Less Than

All numbers have a certain 1._____. So some numbers are greater than others. And some numbers are less than others.

A number that comes after another number is 2._____ than it. For example, 6 comes after 5. So we can say, "6 is greater than 5." In math 3._____, we write it like this: 6 > 5. A number that comes before another number is 4._____ than it. For example, 2 comes before 3. So we can say, "2 is less than 3." In math terms, we write it like this: 2 < 3.

B Read the passage above and answer the following questions.

_____ 5. What is closest to the main point the author wants to make?

     a Some numbers are greater than other numbers.

     b The greater-than symbol is very hard to write.

     c The number two is less than three.

     d Numbers can be confusing sometimes.

_____ 6. This article focuses on number _____.

     a origins

     b writing

     c values

     d sums

_____ 7. "In math terms, we write it like . . ." In this example, the word "terms" means _____.

     a words used to show a concept

     b addition and subtraction problems

     c casual names for something

     d the backgrounds of numbers

Listen to the passage and fill in the blanks.

🎧 143 | Addition and Subtraction |

Addition is 1._____ two or more numbers together. When you add numbers together, the answer you get is called 2._____. For example, the sum of 5+2 is 7. 3._____ is taking a number 4._____ from another. Imagine you have 5 apples. You take away 2 apples and give them to your brother. How many are 5._____? There were 5 apples, but you took away 2, so now you have 3 apples. 5-2=3. The number you have left is called the 6._____.

So, the difference of 5-2 is 3.

Read the passage above and answer the following questions.

_____ 7. Which statement below best expresses the main idea of this article?
  a Addition is more useful than subtraction.
  b Addition and subtraction are two math skills.
  c It's better to have five apples rather than three.
  d When you add numbers together, you get a sum.

_____ 8. The value separating the two numbers in subtraction is called _____.
  a the sum
  b the remainder
  c the proof
  d the difference

_____ 9. "When you add numbers together, the answer you get is called the sum. " A word with the same meaning as "answer" is _____.
  a success
  b solution
  c factor
  d instruction

Unit 24

A Listen to the passage and fill in the blanks.

🎧144 | **Making Change**

People use 1._____ to buy many different 2._____ and 3._____.
Money can be both paper 4._____ and coins. All bills and coins have different
5._____. Learn to recognize the 6._____ so that you can know how much
they are 7._____. You might buy some candy at a store. It costs seventy-
five 8._____, so you give the clerk a dollar. One 9._____ is worth 100
cents. How much change will you get back? Twenty-five cents. You'll receive one
10._____. But maybe you don't want a quarter. Tell the clerk, "I'd like two
11._____ and a 12._____, please." That is how you make change.

B Read the passage above and answer the following questions.

_____ 13. Which sentence best expresses the main idea of this article?
      a People use money to buy goods and services.
      b Most people save their pennies until they have at least 25.
      c People often buy candy at the store.
      d When you buy things, you can receive change in different coins and bills.

_____ 14. How many cents are in one dollar?
      a 100.
      b 50.
      c 25.
      d 1,000.

_____ 15. "Learn to recognize the coins so that you can know how much they are worth."
      The word "worth" means _____.
      a how old something is
      b how valuable something is
      c how large something is
      d how heavy something is

Unit 25

A Listen to the passage and fill in the blanks.

🎧 145 **A Friendly Letter**

1._____ 31, 2009

Dear John,

My name is Sara.

I live in Seoul,

2._____

Where do you live?

I go to Central

3._____ School.

I like to 4._____

my bike. Please write

me back and tell me

about yourself.

5._____ ,

Sara

Date: Begin with the date at the top. Use a capital letter for the name of the month.

Greeting: Start your greeting with "Dear." Use a capital D.

Capitalization: Use capital letters to begin a sentence.

Question: Use question marks at the end of questions.

Names: Capitalize the names of people, places, and things.

Closing: End the letter with a closing and your name. Use a capital letter to begin the closing and put a comma after the closing.

Don't forget that your name should start with a capital letter, too.

B Read the passage above and answer the following questions.

_____ 6. What is closest to the main point the author wants to make?

        a Everyone writes letters in their own way.

        b Letter writing is popular in South Korea.

        c Sarah misses her friend John.

        d There is a proper way to write a letter.

_____ 7. Which of the following should always be at the top right corner of a letter?

        a The sender's name.   b The weather.

        c The date.   d The word "sincerely."

_____ 8. "Start your greeting with . . ." Which of the following is NOT an example of a greeting?

        a Hello.   b Dear.   c Goodbye.   d How are you?

Unit 26

A Listen to the passage and fill in the blanks.

Aesop's Fables

Aesop was a 1._____ who lived in ancient Greece. He lived more than 2,000 years ago. He is famous because of the 2._____ of stories he told. Today, we call them Aesop's Fables.

Aesop's Fables are short 3._____. Often, animals are the main 4._____. Through the stories about animals, Aesop teaches us how we should act as people. At the end of the 5._____, Aesop always tells us a 6._____. The lesson is called the 7._____ of the story. Many of his stories are still famous today. *The Tortoise and the Hare* is very popular. So is *The Ant and the Grasshopper*. *The Lion and the Mouse* and *The Fox and the Grapes* are also well known.

B Read the passage above and answer the following questions.

_____ 8. Which statement below best expresses the main idea of this article?
   [a] Aesop was born in ancient Greece.
   [b] Aesop invented some very famous fables.
   [c] The Fox and the Grapes is a well-known fable.
   [d] Aesop's stories are known as Aesop's Fables.

_____ 9. Another good title for this article is _____.
   [a] Famous Old Animal Stories
   [b] The Story of the Tortoise and the Hare
   [c] Life in Ancient Greece
   [d] The Early Life of Aesop

_____ 10. "Aesop was a slave who lived in ancient Greece." Something is "ancient" is not _____.
   [a] new   [b] aged
   [c] old   [d] elderly

Unit 27

Listen to the passage and fill in the blanks.

147 | **Primary and Secondary Colors**

There are three basic 1._____. They are red, yellow, and blue. We call these three 2._____ colors. You can make other colors when you 3._____ these colors together. For example, mix red and yellow to create orange. 4._____ yellow and blue to make green. And you get purple or 5._____ when you mix red and blue together. We call these 6._____ colors. Of course, there are many other colors. You can make black by mixing red, 7._____, and blue all together. You can also mix primary and secondary colors to get other colors.

B **Read the passage above and answer the following questions.**

_____ 8. Which sentence best expresses the main idea of this article?
   a Primary colors can be mixed to make lots of different colors.
   b You get purple when you mix red and blue together.
   c There are more primary colors than secondary colors.
   d Orange is known as a secondary color.

_____ 9. "You can make other colors when you mix these colors together." The word "mix" means to _____.
   a make something clean
   b study
   c combine things
   d take away

_____ 10. "There are three basic colors." A word with a similar meaning to "basic" is _____.
   a hard   b bright
   c simple   d rare

Listen to the passage and fill in the blanks.

🎧 148 | **Famous Painters**

Art galleries 1._____ the works of lots of painters. There have been many 2._____. Some of them are very famous. 3._____ make many different kinds of paintings. But they are all beautiful in their own way.

Picasso was a famous 4._____ painter. Manet, Monet, Cezanne, and van Gogh painted more than 100 years ago. Leonardo da Vinci was very famous also. He painted the most famous 5._____ in the world: the *Mona Lisa*. Rembrandt was a painter from a long time ago. So was Michelangelo. He painted 6._____ 500 years ago.

B **Read the passage above and answer the following questions.**

_____ 7. What is closest to the main point the author wants to make?
- a Art galleries are beautiful places.
- b Painters are important people.
- c It's expensive to paint.
- d There have been many painters.

_____ 8. According to the article, who is NOT a painter who painted more than 100 years ago?
- a Manet.
- b Monet.
- c Picasso.
- d Cezanne.

_____ 9. The article mentions that Leonardo da Vinci "painted the most famous portrait in the world. A "portrait" is a _____.
- a photograph of a painting
- b picture of a person
- c drawing of scenery
- d place where art is shown

Unit 29

A Listen to the passage and fill in the blanks.

 149

Musicians and Their Musical Instruments

There are so many kinds of musical 1._____. They make many different sounds. So there are also many kinds of music. 2._____ musicians often use the guitar and 3._____. Jazz music needs a 4._____ and saxophone. And 5._____ music uses many various kinds of instruments.

People often play two or more instruments together. They do this in a band or an 6._____. But the musicians must all play at the same time. Many of them read 7._____ music. This tells them what 8._____ to play. If they play well together, they create a 9._____ sound.

B Read the passage above and answer the following questions.

_____ 10. Which sentence best expresses the main idea of this article?
  a Sheet music tells musicians what to play.
  b Different instruments create different music.
  c Musicians must play at the same time.
  d Rock musicians prefer the guitar.

_____ 11. Which type of music relies on the musical instrument called a saxophone?
  a Rock music.
  b Jazz music.
  c Classical music.
  d Harmonious music.

_____ 12. "They do this in a band or an orchestra." An "orchestra" is _____.
  a a concert hall
  b a musical instrument store
  c a large group of musicians
  d a type of music

Listen to the passage and fill in the blanks.

150 **Popular Children's Songs**

What makes a song 1._____? There are many factors involved. Often, the 2._____ songs are the most popular with people. The words to the song might be easy, so people can remember them easily. Or the 3._____ is easy to play or remember, so people often 4._____ or whistle the music.

Some songs are well-liked by young people. *Bingo* is one of these songs. *Old MacDonald* is another, and so are *Twinkle, Twinkle, Little Star* and *La Cucaracha*. Why do people like them? The words often 5._____, the words, and the 6._____ are catchy.

Read the passage above and answer the following questions.

_____ 7. What is closest to the main point the author wants to make?

a Some songs are particularly popular with children.

b If the words of a song repeat, it will become popular.

c The words of a song should always rhyme.

d Children don't listen to a lot of music.

_____ 8. Which of the following is NOT mentioned as a reason people like certain songs?

a The music is easy to play.

b The words rhyme.

c The title is easy to remember.

d The tune is catchy.

_____ 9. The article mentions that certain tunes are catchy. Another word for "catchy" as it is used in this article is _____.

a silent

b similar

c confusing

d memorable

Answer Key

Unit 01
1 neighbors 2 community 3 care about 4 greet
5 Get to know 6 respect 7 privacy 8 a 9 c 10 b

Unit 02
1 elementary 2 class 3 homeroom 4 Pledge
5 Allegiance 6 cafeteria 7 recess 8 c 9 b 10 c

Unit 03
1 customs 2 cultures 3 respect 4 Asian
5 take off 6 forks 7 knives 8 d 9 c 10 a

Unit 04
1 president 2 government 3 elected 4 officials
5 senators 6 representatives 7 laws 8 b 9 d 10 a

Unit 05
1 Christianity 2 holidays 3 Christmas 4 Easter
5 celebrate 6 dead 7 church 8 b 9 c 10 d

Unit 06
1 protected 2 damage 3 stunning 4 scenery
5 canyons 6 hiking 7 preserve 8 b 9 a 10 a

Unit 07
1 continents 2 Asia 3 Europe 4 Africa 5 Australia
6 Pacific 7 Atlantic 8 Indian 9 b 10 a 11 b

Unit 08
1 Maps 2 drawings 3 neighborhoods 4 continents
5 countries 6 details 7 individual 8 b 9 a 10 a

Unit 09
1 species 2 endangered 3 die 4 extinct
5 hunting 6 set aside 7 live on 8 a 9 b 10 d

Unit 10
1 New World 2 explorers 3 cruel 4 war 5 natives
6 defeated 7 slaves 8 treasure 9 b 10 a 11 a

Unit 11
1 seasons 2 spring 3 fall 4 winter 5 autumn
6 weather 7 rainy 8 bloom 9 sunny 10 temperature
11 snows 12 a 13 b 14 c

Unit 12
1 plants 2 soil 3 sunlight 4 nutrients 5 stems
6 leaves 7 blossom 8 c 9 b 10 a

Unit 13
1 habitat 2 survive 3 live in 4 desert 5 forest
6 unique 7 temperature 8 shelter 9 c 10 b 11 a

Unit 14
1 ocean 2 seafood 3 shellfish 4 shrimp 5 clams
6 crabs 7 lobsters 8 fishermen 9 grounds 10 c
11 a 12 b

Unit 15
1 machine 2 breaks down 3 germs 4 attack
5 defeat 6 medicine 7 a 8 c 9 d

Unit 16
1 solid 2 liquid 3 gas 4 heat 5 ice
6 boils 7 steam 8 vapor 9 b 10 a 11 b

Unit 17
1 ingredients 2 measure 3 flour 4 teaspoons
5 extract 6 soda 7 chips 8 a 9 b 10 a

Unit 18
1 scientist 2 lightning 3 electricity
4 experiment 5 kite 6 flew 7 striking
8 charges 9 electricity 10 d 11 b 12 c

Unit 19
1 solar 2 planets 3 Venus 4 Mars 5 Pluto
6 objects 7 outer 8 b 9 d 10 c

Unit 20
1 crust 2 mantle 3 core 4 surface 5 deserts
6 layers 7 melted 8 liquid 9 c 10 d 11 d

Unit 21
1 shapes 2 square 3 resemble 4 rectangle
5 triangle 6 circles 7 oval 8 pyramid
9 c 10 c 11 d

Unit 22
1 value 2 greater 3 terms 4 less 5 a 6 c 7 a

Unit 23
1 adding 2 sum 3 Subtraction 4 away
5 left 6 difference 7 b 8 d 9 b

Unit 24
1 money 2 goods 3 services 4 bills 5 values
6 coins 7 worth 8 cents 9 dollar 10 quarter
11 dimes 12 nickel 13 d 14 a 15 b

Unit 25
1 August 2 Korea 3 Elementary 4 ride
5 Sincerely 6 d 7 c 8 c

Unit 26
1 slave 2 collection 3 stories 4 characters
5 fable 6 lesson 7 moral 8 b 8 a 10 a

Unit 27
1 colors 2 primary 3 mix 4 Combine 5 violet
6 secondary 7 yellow 8 a 9 c 10 c

Unit 28
1 display 2 painters 3 Artists 4 modern
5 portrait 6 around 7 d 8 c 9 b

Unit 29
1 instruments 3 Rock 3 drums 4 piano
5 classical 6 orchestra 7 sheet 8 notes
9 harmonious 10 b 11 b 12 c

Unit 30
1 popular 2 simplest 3 melody 4 hum
5 repeat 6 rhyme 7 tunes 8 a 9 c 10 d

How to Use This Book

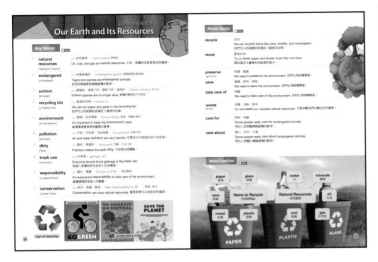

Key Words
熟記和主題有關的10個關鍵字彙，同時也記下該字的例句，並且瀏覽相關補充用語。搭配MP3反覆聽三遍，一直到熟悉字義和發音為止。

Power Verbs
熟記和主題相關的高頻率核心動詞和動詞片語。片語是用簡單的字來表達複雜的涵義，常在TOEFL等國際英語能力測驗中的題目出現，所以要確實地將這些由2-3個字所組成的片語記熟。

Word Families
將容易聯想在一起的字彙或表現形式，以獨特的圈組方式來幫助記憶。這些字就像針線一樣，時常在一起出現，因此要熟知這些字的差異和使用方法。

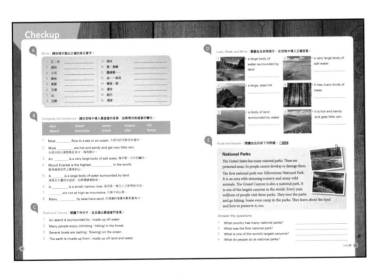

Checkup

A Write｜練習寫出本書所學到的字彙，一方面能夠熟悉單字的拼法，一方面也能夠幫助記憶。

B Complete the Sentences｜將本書所學到的字彙和例句，確實背熟。

C Read and Choose｜透過多樣化的練習，熟悉本書所學到的字彙用法。

D Look, Read, and Write｜透過照片、插畫和提示，加深對所學到的字彙的印象。

E Read and Answer｜透過與各單元主題有關的「文章閱讀理解測驗」，來熟悉教科書的出題模式，並培養與各學科相關的背景知識和適應各種考試的能力。

Review Test 1
每5個單元結束會有一回總複習測驗，有助於回想起沒有辦法一次就記起來或忘記的單字，並且再次複習。

Table of Contents

Introduction
How to Use This Book

Workbook 聽力閱讀試題本

Syllabus Vol.1

Subject	Topic & Area	Title
Social Studies ● **History and Geography**	Citizenship Citizenship Skills Culture American History World History American Geography World Geography Geography Skills World Geography American History	Our Community Home and School Life Different Cultures and Holidays The American Government World Religions Our Land and Water Oceans and Continents Maps and Directions Our Earth and Its Resources Native Americans and Europeans in the New World
Science	Seasons and Weather Plants and Animal A World of Living Things A World of Living Things The Human Body Exploring Matter Measurement Electricity The Solar System Our Earth	Seasons and Weather The Parts of a Plant Homes for Living Things Oceans and Undersea Life The Human Body How Can Matter Change? How Long? How Tall? Electricity Our Solar System Inside the earth
Mathematics	Geometry Numbers and Number Sense Computation Money	Shapes Numbers and Counting Addition and Subtraction Counting Money
Language and Literature	Learning about Language Learning about Language	Read and Write Types of Writing
Visual Arts	Painting Painting	A World of Lines and Colors A World of Paintings
Music	Musical Instruments A World of Music	Instruments and Their Families A World of Music

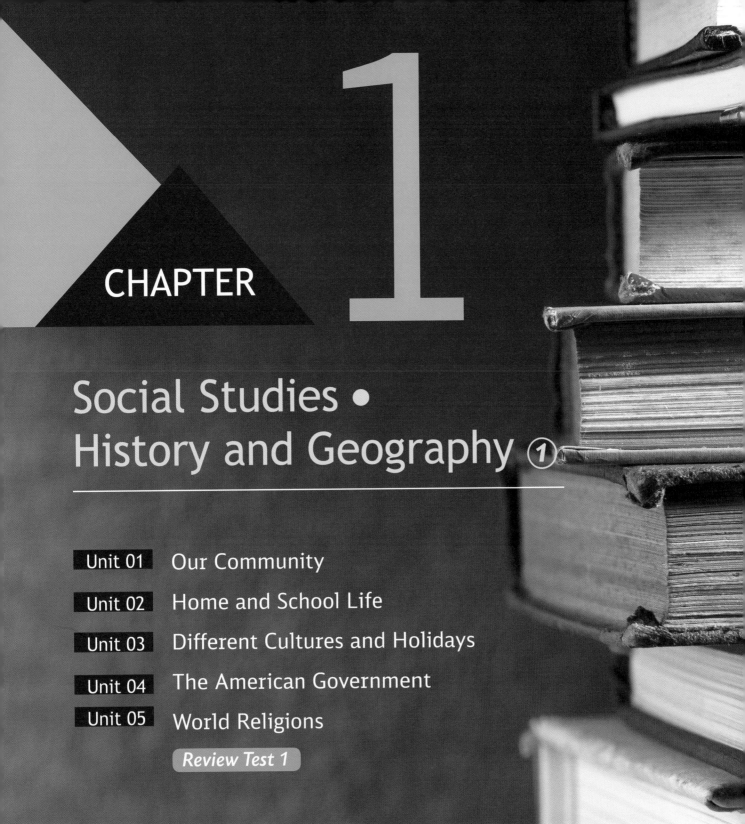

CHAPTER 1

Social Studies •
History and Geography ①

Our Community 社區環境

Key Words 🔊 001

01 neighborhood
[ˈnebəˌhʊd]
(n.) 鄰近地區；整個街坊；鄰里情誼　*neighbor 鄰居；鄰國
A **neighborhood** is a place where people live together.
人們住在一起的地方稱為街坊。

02 community
[kəˈmjunətɪ]
(n.) 社區；共同體　*business community 工商界
In our **community**, people help each other and care about one another.
在我們的共同社會中，人們會互相幫忙、彼此照應。

03 city
[ˈsɪtɪ]
(n.) 城市　*major city 主要城市
A **city** is a big community. 城市是一個大社區。

04 suburb
[ˈsʌbɝb]
(n.) 郊區　*urban area 市區
Suburbs are small cities near a big city. 郊區是在大都市旁邊的小城市。

05 state
[stet]
(n.) 州　*state law 州法
There are fifty **states** in the United States. 美國有 50 州。

06 country
[ˈkʌntrɪ]
(n.) 國家；鄉下　*foreign country 外國　*developing country 開發中國家
How many **countries** are there in the world? 世界上共有幾個國家？

07 community center
[kəˈmjunətɪ ˈsɛntɚ]
(n.) 社區活動中心
People can do many activities at a **community center**.
人們可以在社區活動中心從事許多活動。

08 leader
[ˈlidɚ]
(n.) 領導者；領袖　*leadership 領導地位／身分
A mayor is the **leader** of a community. 市長是一個共同社會的領導人。

09 citizen
[ˈsɪtəzn̩]
(n.) 市民；公民　*senior citizen 老年人
A good **citizen** treats others with respect. 良好的公民會彼此尊重。

10 citizenship
[ˈsɪtəzn̩ˌʃɪp]
(n.) 公民權　*dual citizenship 雙重國籍
Citizenship is being a good member of a community.
公民權就是要成為共同社會中良好的一員。

community

neighborhood

neighbor

take　乘（車）；搭（船）
Many people **take** the bus to work or school.
許多人搭公車去上班或上學。

ride on　騎坐
Many people **ride on** the bus to work or school.
許多人坐公車上班或上學。

live　住
People in cities often **live** in apartment buildings. 都市人通常都住在公寓大樓裡。

reside [rɪˈzaɪd]　居住
People in cities often **reside** in apartment buildings.
都市人通常都居住在公寓大樓裡。

get to know　認識
Neighbors often **get to know** each other. 鄰居通常都彼此互相認識。

get along with　與……相處
Neighbors often **get along with** each other. 鄰居通常都彼此和睦相處。

be close to　與……親近
Neighbors **are** often **close to** each other. 鄰居通常都彼此親近。

Streets 街道	**Transportation** 交通工具	**Places Around Town** 市區地標
road 路；道路 Oxford Rd. 牛津路	**bus** 公車	**bank** 銀行
street 街道 York St. 約克街	**subway** 地下鐵	**post office** 郵局
avenue 大街；大道 Park Ave. 公園大道	**train** 火車	**fire station** 消防局
boulevard 大馬路 Hollywood Blvd. 好萊塢大道	**commuter train** 通勤火車	**police station** 警察局
	taxi 計程車	**city hall** 市政廳
	car 汽車	**library** 圖書館
	motorcycle 摩托車	**hospital** 醫院
	bicycle 腳踏車	**supermarket** 超級市場

Checkup

A Write | 請依提示寫出正確的英文單字。

1	鄰近地區	_____	9	郵局 _____
2	社區	_____	10	公民權 _____
3	城市	_____	11	乘(車)；搭(船) _____
4	郊區	_____	12	騎坐 _____
5	領導者	_____	13	居住 r_____
6	州	_____	14	認識 _____
7	國家	_____	15	大街；大道 a_____
8	公民	_____	16	交通工具 _____

B Complete the Sentences | 請在空格中填入最適當的答案，並視情況做適當的變化。

neighborhood	leader	citizen	citizenship	take
community center	state	country	get along	ride

1 A _____ is a place where people live together.
人們住在一起的地方稱為街坊。

2 A good _____ treats others with respect. 良好的公民會彼此尊重。

3 A mayor is the _____ of a community. 市長是一個共同社會的領導人。

4 _____ is being a good member of a community.
公民權就是要成為共同社會中良好的一員。

5 Neighbors often _____ _____ with each other. 鄰居通常都彼此和睦相處。

6 Many people _____ the bus to work or school. 許多人搭公車去上班或上學。

7 People can do many activities at a _____ _____.
人們可以在社區活動中心從事許多活動。

8 How many _____ are there in the world? 世界上共有幾個國家？

C Read and Choose | 閱讀下列句子，並且選出最適當的答案。

1 (States | Suburbs) are small cities near a big city.

2 A (city | suburb) is a big community.

3 There are fifty (states | countries) in the United States.

4 People in cities often (ride | reside) in apartment buildings.

D Look, Read, and Write | 看圖並且依照提示，在空格中填入正確答案。

1 ▶ a place where people live together

_____

4 ▶ a person who leads a community

_____

2 ▶ small cities near a big city

_____

5 ▶ a building used by members of a community for social events

_____

3 ▶ a big community such as New York

_____

6 ▶ a member of a town, state, or country

_____

E Read and Answer | 閱讀並且回答下列問題。 `004`

Good Neighbors

Your neighbors are the people who live near you. In our community, people help each other and care about one another. If you want to have a good neighbor, you have to be a good neighbor first. There are many ways to do this. First, you can be nice to your neighbors. Always greet them and say, "Hello." Get to know them. Become friends with them. Also, don't be noisy at your home. And respect your neighbors' privacy. If they have any problems, help them out. They will help you too in the future. If you do all of these things, you can be a good neighbor.

Fill in the blanks.

1   _____ are people who live near you.

2   You should always be _____ to your neighbors.

3   Try to respect your neighbors' _____.

4   Good neighbors often _____ their neighbors out.

Key Words 🔊 005

01 manners
['mænəz]

(n.)〔複〕禮貌；規矩；風俗習慣　*manner〔單〕方式；方法
Children need to have good **manners**. 孩子必須要有良好的規矩。

02 behavior
[bɪˈhevjə]

(n.) 行為　*good behavior 品行良好
Students should always be on their best **behavior**.
學生應該隨時都要有最好的表現。

03 rule
[rul]

(n.) 規定　*as a general rule 一般地；大體上
There are many **rules** at home and school. 家裡和學校有許多規定。

04 homeroom
['hom,rum]

(n.)（召集年級活動時使用的）大教室　*school hall 學校禮堂
Students go to their **homeroom** in the morning.
學生們早上到大教室裡。

05 class
[klæs]

(n.) 一節課；班級；階級　*classmate 同班同學
Students are taught different things in each **class**.
學生們每堂課都學到不同的東西。

06 hallway
['hɔl,we]

(n.) 走廊；玄關；門廳　*hall 會堂；大廳　*doorway 門口
Do not run in the **hallway**. 不要在走廊上奔跑。

07 playground
['ple,graund]

(n.) 操場；運動場；遊樂場所　*school yard 校園；運動場
There are seesaws and slides on the **playground**.
運動場上有翹翹板和溜滑梯。

08 get along
[gɛt əˈlɔŋ]

(v.) 和睦相處；進展　*get on with sb. 與某人和睦相處
We should always **get along** with our classmates.
我們應該要與同學和睦相處。

09 activity
[ækˈtɪvətɪ]

(n.) 活動　*active (a.) 活潑的
Art class is full of many fun **activities**. 美術課充滿了許多有趣的活動。

10 recess
[rɪˈsɛs]

(n.) 課間休息；學校的假期　*break (n.) 休息時間
The students play games during **recess**. 學生在下課時間玩遊戲。

class

recess

Pledge of Allegiance

follow	跟隨;聽從	
	You should **follow** all the rules. 你應該遵守所有的規定。	
obey [ə`be]	遵守;聽從	
	You should **obey** all the rules. 你應該遵守所有的規定。	

listen	注意聽;聽從
	Always **listen** to your parents. 要永遠聽從父母的話。
pay attention	關心;注意
	Always **pay attention** to your parents. 要永遠關心你的父母。

recite [ri`saɪt]	背誦;朗誦
	Students **recite** the Pledge of Allegiance every morning.
	學生每天早上都會朗誦「忠誠宣誓」。
state	陳述;說明
	Students **state** the Pledge of Allegiance every morning.
	學生每天早上都會陳述「忠誠宣誓」。

*Pledge of Allegiance 美國中小學每天都有一種宣示儀式,宣誓的內容為全國通用,或是自己所
在的州的誓言。

Word Families ● 007

Some School Rules 一些校規	**Good Behavior** 良好的行為	**Bad Behavior** 不好的行為
Raise your hand to talk. 舉手發言。 **Do not run in the hallways.** 不要在走廊上奔跑。 **Be quiet in class.** 上課安靜。 **Play ball outside.** 玩球要到室外。	**listening to teachers** 聽從老師的話 **obeying the rules** 遵守規定 **studying** 讀書 **trying** 嘗試	**running in the hallway** 在走廊上奔跑 **fighting** 打架 **yelling** 大吼大叫 **screaming** 尖叫 **spitting** 吐口水 **cheating** 作弊

Checkup

A Write | 請依提示寫出正確的英文單字。

1	禮貌	_____	9	大教室	_____
2	行為	_____	10	和睦相處	_____
3	規定	_____	11	注意聽；聽從	_____
4	一節課	_____	12	背誦；朗誦	_____
5	走廊	_____	13	陳述；說明	_____
6	活動	_____	14	跟隨；聽從	_____
7	運動場	_____	15	關心；注意	_____
8	課間休息	_____	16	忠誠宣誓	_____

B Complete the Sentences | 請在空格中填入最適當的答案，並視情況做適當的變化。

rule	hallway	manners	homeroom	class
recess	behavior	activity	playground	listen

1 There are many _____ at home and school. 家裡和學校有許多規定。

2 Students should always be on their best _____.
學生應該隨時都要有最好的表現。

3 Students are taught different things in each _____.
學生們每堂課都學到不同的東西。

4 Children need to have good _____. 孩子必須要有良好的規矩。

5 There are seesaws and slides on the _____. 運動場上有翹翹板和溜滑梯。

6 The students play games during _____. 學生在下課時間玩遊戲。

7 Art class is full of many fun _____. 美術課充滿了許多有趣的活動。

8 Students go to their _____ in the morning. 學生們早上到大教室裡。

C Read and Choose | 請選出與鋪底字意思相近的答案。

1 Always listen to your parents.

   a. obey   b. pay attention   c. state

2 Students recite the Pledge of Allegiance every morning.

   a. state   b. remember   c. obey

3 You should follow all the rules.

   a. listen to   b. pay attention to   c. obey

D

Complete the rules.

1  ▶ _____ your hand to talk.

4  ▶ Play ball _____.

2  ▶ Do not _____.

5  ▶ _____ to your teachers.

3  ▶ Be _____ in class.

6  ▶ _____ with your classmates.

E

Read and Answer | 閱讀並且回答下列問題。 🔊 008

A Day at School

John and Sally go to elementary school. Their first class starts at 8 a.m. They go to their homeroom. They stand up, face the flag, and say the Pledge of Allegiance before their class begins. Then their teacher, Mrs. Smith, starts their lessons. They study math, social studies, English, and art, and then they go to the cafeteria for lunch. After lunch, they have recess, so all the students go outside and play for a while. Then they learn science, history, and music. Finally, it's 3 o'clock. It's time for them to go home!

What is true? Write T (true) or F (false).

1   John and Sally start school at nine.   _____

2   John and Sally's homeroom teacher is Mrs. Smith.   _____

3   John and Sally study math and art before lunch.   _____

4   John and Sally study science and social studies after lunch.   _____

Different Cultures and Holidays

Key Words
⊙ 009

01	**culture** [ˋkʌltʃə]	*(n.)* 文化;修養　*culture shock 文化衝擊 Every country has its own **culture**. 每個國家都有自己的文化。
02	**holiday** [ˋhɑləˏde]	*(n.)* 節日;(國定)假日　*vacation(泛指任何長期的)休假;假期 Christmas is a popular **holiday**. 聖誕節是一個很受歡迎的節日。
03	**favorite** [ˋfevərɪt]	*(a.)* 最喜愛的　*in favor of 支持 My **favorite** holiday is Thanksgiving. 我最喜歡的節日是感恩節。
04	**custom** [ˋkʌstəm]	*(n.)* 社會習俗;個人習慣　*customs〔複〕海關　* 相似形字:costume 戲服 What **customs** do you have on Chinese New Year? 過農曆新年時你們有哪些習俗呢?
05	**tradition** [trəˋdɪʃən]	*(n.)* 傳統;慣例　*ritual 慣例;例行公事 In some countries, it is a **tradition** to go to church on Christmas. 在某些國家,聖誕節當天上教堂是一種傳統。
06	**pride** [praɪd]	*(n.)* 驕傲;自豪　*be proud of 為……感到驕傲 Most citizens have **pride** in their country. 大部分的市民都會為自己的國家感到驕傲。
07	**respect** [rɪˋspɛkt]	*(v.)* 尊重;尊敬　*show respect for 對……表示尊敬 You should always **respect** other cultures. 你應該要一直尊重其他文化。
08	**honor** [ˋɑnə]	*(v.)* 給……以榮譽　*(n.)* 榮譽;名譽;光榮的事或人 *It's my great honor to 我很榮幸…… Memorial Day **honors** the people who died for our country. 陣亡將士紀念日是為了向那些為國捐軀的人致意。
09	**ancestor** [ˋænsɛstə]	*(n.)* 祖先;原型;先驅　*descendant 子孫 People in some cultures honor their **ancestors**. 有些文化的人尊敬他們的祖先。
10	**ceremony** [ˋsɛrəˏmonɪ]	*(n.)* 儀式;典禮;禮儀;禮節;客套 *opening/closing ceremony 開幕/閉幕典禮 They hold a special **ceremony** for their ancestors. 他們為祖先舉行了一場特殊的典禮。

American Holidays

Memorial Day
(5 月的最後一個星期一)

Independence Day
(7月4日)

Thanksgiving Day
(11月的最後一個星期四)

Christmas
(12 月 25 日)

Power Verbs 🔊 010

give 送給；給予
On Christmas, people decorate Christmas trees and **give** gifts.
聖誕節那天，人們會裝飾聖誕樹和送禮物。

receive [rɪ`siv] 收到；得到
On Christmas, people often **receive** presents. 聖誕節那天，人們通常會收到禮物。

remember 記得；記住；想起
It is important to **remember** important holidays. 記住重要節日是很重要的事情。

recall 回想；回憶
It is important to **recall** important holidays. 回憶起重要節日是很重要的事情。

celebrate 慶祝
[`sɛlə,bret]
Families often **celebrate** Thanksgiving together. 家人通常會聚在一起慶祝感恩節。

hold 舉行
The family will **hold** a special ceremony tonight.
這一家人今晚會舉行一場特殊的典禮。

Word Families 🔊 011

Holidays 節慶

Christmas 聖誕節

Easter 復活節

Thanksgiving Day 感恩節

New Year's Day 新年

Independence Day 獨立紀念日

Veterans Day 退伍軍人節

Memorial Day 陣亡將士紀念日

Labor Day 勞工節

Columbus Day 哥倫布日

Valentine's Day 情人節

Money Around the World 各國貨幣

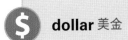 **dollar** 美金

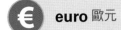 **euro** 歐元

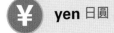 **yen** 日圓

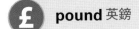 **pound** 英鎊

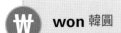 **won** 韓圓

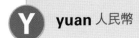 **yuan** 人民幣

Checkup

A

Write | 請依提示寫出正確的英文單字。

1	文化	_____	9	尊重；尊敬	_____
2	節日	_____	10	榮譽；名譽	_____
3	社會習俗	_____	11	送給；給予	_____
4	傳統	_____	12	收到；得到	_____
5	驕傲	_____	13	記得；記住	_____
6	祖先	_____	14	回想；回憶	_____
7	典禮	_____	15	慶祝	_____
8	最喜愛的	_____	16	舉行	_____

B

Complete the Sentences | 請在空格中填入最適當的答案，並視情況做適當的變化。

pride	custom	celebrate	favorite	ancestor
culture	remember	tradition	holiday	ceremony

1 Every country has its own _____. 每個國家都有自己的文化。

2 What _____ do you have on Chinese New Year?
   過農曆新年時你們有哪些習俗呢？

3 My _____ holiday is Thanksgiving. 我最喜歡的節日是感恩節。

4 People in some cultures honor their _____.
   有些文化的人尊敬他們的祖先。

5 They hold a special _____ for their ancestors.
   他們為了祖先舉行了一場特殊的典禮。

6 Most citizens have _____ in their country.
   大部分的市民都會以自己的國家感到驕傲。

7 It is important to _____ important holidays.
   記住重要節日是很重要的事情。

8 In some countries, it is a _____ to go to church on Christmas.
   在某些國家，聖誕節當天上教堂是一種傳統。

C

Read and Choose | 閱讀下列句子，並且選出最適當的答案。

1 Families often (celebrate | honor) Thanksgiving together.

2 On Christmas, people (celebrate | give) gifts.

3 Memorial Day (honors | holds) the people who died for our country.

4 You should always (recall | respect) other cultures.

D　Look, Read, and Write | 看圖並且依照提示，在空格中填入正確答案。

What's the holiday?

 ► It's celebrated on the 25th of December.

_____

 ► It's the first day of the year.

_____

 ► It's a Christian holiday that celebrates Christ's return to life.

_____

 ► In some countries, couples express their love for each other on this day.

_____

 ► It celebrates the anniversary of a country's freedom from control by another country.

_____

 ► Families get together and eat a big dinner on this day.

_____

E　Read and Answer | 閱讀並且回答下列問題。　🔘 012

Different Customs and Cultures

Americans have their own customs and cultures. But many other countries have these, too. We should know about other people's customs and cultures. And we should always respect them. For example, in America, people wear their shoes in their homes. But in some Asian countries like Japan and Korea, people take off their shoes before going inside their homes. And Americans eat with forks and knives. But in India and other countries, people often eat with their hands. There are many other differences. And we should know and learn about them.

Fill in the blanks.

1　Every country has its own customs and _____.

2　Americans wear their _____ in their homes.

3　Americans _____ with forks and knives.

4　People in _____ and other countries often eat with their hands.

Unit 04 The American Government 美國政府

Key Words 🔊 013

| 01 | **capital** | *(n.)* 首都；大寫字母；資金　＊相似形字：Capitol 美國州議會大廈 |
| | [ˈkæpətḷ] | The **capital** of the United States is Washington, D.C.
美國的首都是華盛頓特區。 |

| 02 | **citizen** | *(n.)* 市民；公民　＊citizenship 公民權 |
| | [ˈsɪtəzṇ] | Americans are **citizens** of the United States. 美國人是美國的公民。 |

| 03 | **election** | *(n.)* 選舉；當選　＊presidential election 總統選舉 |
| | [ɪˈlɛkʃən] | Many people vote in **elections**. 多數人會在選舉中投票。 |

| 04 | **vote** | *(n.)* 投票；選票 *(v.)* 投票　＊ballot 選票；投票用紙 |
| | [vot] | Each person gets one **vote**. 每個人都有一張選票。 |

| 05 | **government** | *(n.)* 政府；政體　＊authorities 官方；當局　＊local government 地方政府 |
| | [ˈgʌvənmənt] | The president is the leader of the **government**. 總統是政府的領導人。 |

| 06 | **law** | *(n.)* 法律；定律　＊to practice law 從事律師工作 |
| | [lɔ] | **Laws** tell people what they can and cannot do.
法律讓人民了解到何種行為可為或不可為。 |

| 07 | **right** | *(n.)* 權利　＊human right 人權 |
| | [raɪt] | All citizens have certain **rights**. 全體公民都享有特定之權利。 |

| 08 | **freedom** | *(n.)* 自由　＊academic freedom 學術自由 |
| | [ˈfridəm] | Americans have **freedom** of speech and religion.
美國人民享有言論和宗教自由。 |

| 09 | **symbol** | *(n.)* 符號；象徵　＊a symbol of ……的象徵 |
| | [ˈsɪmbḷ] | The bald eagle is a **symbol** of the United States. 白頭鷹是美國的象徵。 |

| 10 | **flag** | *(n.)* 旗　＊to flag up 引起注意 |
| | [flæg] | The American **flag** has 13 stripes and 50 stars.
美國國旗上有 13 道條紋和 50 顆星。（代表 50 個州和建國時的 13 處殖民地） |

American Symbols

the Statue of Liberty

the Capitol Building

the White House

elect
選舉
Americans **elect** a president every four years. 美國人民每四年會選出一位總統。

vote
投票；選舉；投票權
Americans 18 or older can **vote** in elections.
18 歲以上的美國人在選舉中具有投票權。

protect
保護；防護
The president's job is to **protect** the country. 總統的職責在於保護國家。

defend
防禦；保護；保衛
The president's job is to **defend** the country. 總統的職責在於保衛國家。

govern
統治；管理
A president **governs** a country. 總統治理一個國家。

rule
統治；支配
A king **rules** a country. 國王統治一個國家。

symbolize
['sɪmbḷˌaɪz]
象徵
The Statue of Liberty **symbolizes** freedom. 自由女神像象徵著自由。

stand for
代表；象徵
The Statue of Liberty **stands for** freedom. 自由女神像代表著自由。

Word Families ● 015

Government Officials 政府官員	**American Symbols** 美國的象徵
president 總統 **senator** 參議員 **representative** 眾議員 **governor** 州長 **mayor** 市長	**the American flag** 美國國旗 **the bald eagle** 白頭鷹 **the Statue of Liberty** 自由女神像 **the White House** 白宮 **the Capitol Building** 國會大廈

Checkup

A Write | 請依提示寫出正確的英文單字。

1	首都	_____	9	符號；象徵 (n.) _____
2	市民；公民	_____	10	旗 _____
3	選舉；當選 (n.)	_____	11	選舉 (v.) _____
4	投票；選票	_____	12	政府官員 _____
5	法律	_____	13	保護；防護 _____
6	權利	_____	14	防禦 _____
7	自由	_____	15	統治；管理 g_____
8	政府	_____	16	象徵 (v.) _____

B Complete the Sentences | 請在空格中填入最適當的答案，並視情況做適當的變化。

elect	freedom	capital	law	citizen
vote	election	flag	right	government

1 Americans are _____ of the United States. 美國人是美國的公民。

2 The _____ of the United States is Washington, D.C. 美國的首都是華盛頓特區。

3 All citizens have certain _____. 全體公民都享有特定之權利。

4 Americans have _____ of speech and religion. 美國人民享有言論和宗教自由。

5 _____ tell people what they can and cannot do.
法律讓人民了解到何種行為可為或不可為。

6 The president is the leader of the _____. 總統是政府的領導人。

7 Americans _____ a president every four years. 美國人民每四年會選出一位總統。

8 Many people vote in _____. 多數人會在選舉中投票。

C

Read and Choose | 請選出與鋪底字意思相近的答案。

1 The Statue of Liberty symbolizes freedom.
   a. protects   b. defends   c. stands for

2 The president's job is to protect the country.
   a. defend   b. elect   c. vote

3 A president governs a country.
   a. rules   b. stands for   c. makes

D Look, Read, and Write | 看圖並且依照提示，在空格中填入正確答案。

What is this?

 1
▶ It symbolizes freedom.
_____

 4
▶ The members of Congress work here.
_____

 2
▶ It has 13 stripes and 50 stars.
_____

 5
▶ It is a symbol of the U.S.
_____

 3
▶ a person who is elected to lead a city
_____

 6
▶ It is the capital of the U.S.
_____

E Read and Answer | 閱讀並且回答下列問題。 🔊 016

The Leaders of the American Government

The president is the leader of the American government. He is elected by the people and serves for four years. He lives in the White House. There are other government officials, too. Many serve in Congress. Congress is divided into two parts. They are the Senate and the House of Representatives. Every state has two senators. And every state has a different number of representatives in the House. Some have many. But some have just one or two. The members of Congress make all the laws for the country. They work from the Capitol in Washington, D.C.

Answer the questions.

1 Who leads the American government? _____
2 Where does the president live? _____
3 How many senators does each state have? _____
4 Where does Congress work? _____

Unit 05 World Religions 世界宗教

Key Words 🔊 017

01	**religion** [rɪˈlɪdʒən]	(n.) 宗教；宗教信仰　*follow/practice a religion 信仰宗教 There are many **religions** in the world. 世界上有許多宗教。
02	**Christianity** [ˌkrɪstʃɪˈænətɪ]	(n.) 基督教　*Christian 基督教徒 Believers in **Christianity** think that Jesus was the son of God. 基督教徒認為耶穌是上帝的兒子。
03	**Judaism** [ˈdʒudɪˌɪzəm]	(n.) 猶太教　*Jew 猶太教徒 The followers of **Judaism** are called Jews. 猶太教的信徒稱為猶太教徒。
04	**Islam** [ˈɪsləm]	(n.) 伊斯蘭教　*Muslim 伊斯蘭教徒；穆斯林 The god of **Islam** is called Allah. 回教的神稱為阿拉。
05	**Buddhism** [ˈbudɪzəm]	(n.) 佛教　*Buddha 佛陀　*Buddhist 佛教徒 **Buddhism** is a religion with many followers in Asia. 佛教是一種在亞洲擁有許多信徒的宗教。
06	**Hinduism** [ˈhɪnduˌɪzəm]	(n.) 印度教　*Hindu 印度人；印度教徒 Most of **Hinduism**'s followers live in India. 大部分的印度教徒都住在印度。
07	**holy book** [ˈholɪ bʊk]	(n.) 聖典 The *Bible*, *Torah*, and *Koran* are all **holy books**. 《聖經》、《摩西五書》和《可蘭經》都是聖典。
08	**belief** [bɪˈlif]	(n.) 相信；信仰；信念　*in the belief that 相信；認為 People must have **belief** in order to follow a religion. 人一定要懷有信念才能夠追隨宗教。
09	**prayer** [prɛr]	(n.) 禱告；祈願；祈禱者　*answer someone's prayers 回應某人的祈禱 Many people spend time in **prayer** to their god. 很多人都會花時間向神禱告。
10	**priest** [prist]	(n.) (基督教)牧師；(天主教)神父；神職人員　*high priest 大祭司 A Christian **priest** conducts services in church. 基督教牧師服務於教堂。

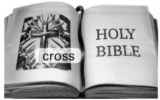
the Bible / cross / HOLY BIBLE
Christianity

menorah / Star of David
Judaism

Buddha
Buddhism

worship in a mosque
Islam

believe in	信仰；信任 Many people **believe in** their religion. 許多人都信仰宗教。
have faith in	信任 Many people **have faith in** their religion. 許多人都相信宗教。
pray	祈禱；祈求 People usually **pray** in church. 人們通常都會上教堂禱告。
worship	信奉；崇拜 People go to church to **worship** God. 人們到教堂裡敬拜上帝。
follow	跟隨；信奉；仿效 Millions of people **follow** the teachings of Jesus. 上百萬人民信奉耶穌的教義。
spread	散佈；傳播 Missionaries **spread** Christianity all over the world. 傳教士將基督教傳播至世界各地。

Word Families 🔊 019

follower	追隨者；信徒；擁護者 There are many **followers** of that religion. 那個宗教擁有許多追隨者。
believer	信徒；信教者 There are many **believers** in that religion. 那個宗教擁有許多信徒。

Believers
信徒

Christian 基督教徒

Jew 猶太教徒

Muslim 穆斯林

Buddhist 佛教徒

Hindu 印度教徒

Places of Worship 敬神之地

church 教堂

mosque 清真寺
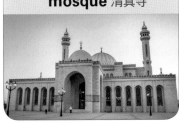

synagogue 猶太教堂

temple 寺廟

Checkup

A

Write | 請依提示寫出正確的英文單字。

1	宗教	_____	9	禱告；祈禱者	_____
2	基督教	_____	10	牧師；神父	_____
3	猶太教	_____	11	佛教徒	_____
4	回教	_____	12	禱告；祈求	_____
5	佛教	_____	13	信奉；崇拜	_____
6	印度教	_____	14	跟隨；信奉	_____
7	聖書	_____	15	追隨者；信徒	_____
8	信仰	_____	16	散布；傳播	_____

B

Complete the Sentences | 請在空格中填入最適當的答案，並視情況做適當的變化。

Hinduism's	follow	belief	religion	pray
Judaism's	Christianity's	believe in	prayer	spread

1 There are many _____ in the world. 世界上有許多宗教。

2 Millions of people _____ the teachings of Jesus.
上百萬人民信奉耶穌的教義。

3 Most of _____ followers live in India. 大部分的印度教徒都住在印度。

4 Many people spend time in _____ to their god.
很多人都會花時間向神禱告。

5 People must have _____ in order to follow a religion.
人一定要懷有信念才能夠追隨宗教。

6 Many people _____ ____ their religion. 許多人都信仰宗教。

7 People usually _____ in church. 人們通常都會上教堂禱告。

8 Missionaries _____ Christianity all over the world.
傳教士將基督教傳播至世界各地。

C

Read and Choose | 閱讀下列句子，並且選出最適當的答案。

1 Believers in (Christianity | Islam) think that Jesus was the son of God.

2 The god of (Hinduism | Islam) is called Allah.

3 (Buddhism | Judaism) is a religion with many followers in Asia.

4 The *Bible*, *Torah*, and *Koran* are all (beliefs | holy books).

D Look, Read, and Write | 看圖並且依照提示，在空格中填入正確答案。

 ▸ believers in
Christianity
_____

 ▸ the followers of
Buddhism
_____

 ▸ the followers of
Judaism
_____

 ▸ the followers of
Hinduism
_____

 ▸ the followers of
Islam
_____

 ▸ a system of beliefs
in a god that has its
own traditions
_____

E

Read and Answer | 閱讀並且回答下列問題。　● 020

Christian Holidays

Christians are people who believe in Christianity.
They believe that Jesus Christ is the son of God.
In Christianity, there are two very important
holidays. They are Christmas and Easter.
Christmas is on December 25. Christians celebrate
the birth of Jesus on this day. Christmas is a time of happiness and celebration.
Easter is in late March or early April every year. It is the most important
Christian holiday. It is the day when Jesus Christ came back from the dead.
Most Christians go to church on this day.

What is NOT true?

1   Christians believe that Jesus Christ is the son of God.

2   Easter is on December 25.

3   Jesus was born on Christmas Day.

4   Easter is the most important Christian holiday.

Review Test 1

A

Write | 請依提示寫出正確的英文單字。

1	鄰近地區	_____	11 鄰居；鄰國	_____
2	社區	_____	12 市民；公民	_____
3	禮貌；規矩	_____	13 和睦相處	_____
4	行為	_____	14 尊重；尊敬	_____
5	規定	_____.	15 榮譽；名譽	_____
6	文化	_____	16 選舉 (v.)	e_____
7	節日；假日	_____	17 投票	_____
8	自由	_____	18 基督教	_____
9	政府	_____	19 猶太教	_____
10	宗教	_____	20 伊斯蘭教	_____

B

Choose the Correct Word | 請選出與鋪底字意思相近的答案。

1 You should **follow** all the rules.

   a. listen to   b. pay attention to   c. obey

2 The Statue of Liberty **symbolizes** freedom.

   a. protects   b. defends   c. stands for

3 The president's job is to **protect** the country.

   a. defend   b. elect   c. vote

4 A president **governs** a country.

   a. rules   b. stands for   c. makes

C

Complete the Sentences | 請在空格中填入最適當的答案，並視情況做適當的變化。

culture	rule	citizenship	believe in

1 _____ is being a good member of a community.
   公民權就是要成為共同社會中良好的一員。

2 Every country has its own _____. 每個國家都有自己的文化。

3 Many people _____ ____ their religion. 許多人都信仰宗教。

4 There are many _____ at home and school. 家裡和學校有許多規定。

CHAPTER 2

Social Studies •
History and Geography ②

Our Land and Water 土地與水源

Key Words 🔊 021

01	**river** [ˋrɪvɚ]	(n.) 江;河　*riverside 河畔 Most rivers flow to a sea or an ocean. 大部分的河都流向海洋。
02	**lake** [lek]	(n.) 湖泊　*pond 池塘 A lake is a large body of water surrounded by land. 湖是由大量的水組成,四周環繞著陸地。
03	**stream** [strim]	(n.) 小河;溪流　*mainstream(河的)主流 A stream is a small, narrow river. 溪流是一條又小又狹窄的河流。
04	**forest** [ˋfɔrɪst]	(n.) 森林　*national forest 國家森林 A forest has many kinds of trees. 森林裡有許多不同種類的樹。
05	**plain** [plen]	(n.) 草原　*coastal plain 濱海平原 Plains are large, flat lands with grasses. 草原是廣大平坦的草地。
06	**desert** [ˋdɛzɚt]	(n.) 沙漠　*desert habitat 沙漠棲息地 Most deserts are hot and sandy and get very little rain. 大部分的沙漠既熱且多沙,降雨稀少。
07	**mountain** [ˋmaʊntn̩]	(n.) 山　*mountain range 山脈 Mount Everest is the highest mountain in the world. 聖母峰是世界上最高的山。
08	**hill** [hɪl]	(n.) 丘陵;小山　*hilltop 山頂 Hills are not as high as mountains. 丘陵不如山高。
09	**ocean** [ˋoʃən]	(n.) 海洋　*sea 海(面積較 ocean〔洋〕小) An ocean is a very large body of salt water. 海洋是一大片的鹹水。
10	**island** [ˋaɪlənd]	(n.) 島;島嶼　*islander 島民 An island is a body of land surrounded by water. 島嶼是指四周環繞著水的陸地。

river

lake

forest

plain

be surrounded by	圍繞著……
	An island is surrounded by water. 島嶼四周環繞著水。
be made up of	由……組成
	The earth is made up of land and water. 地球是由土地和水所組成的。
climb	攀登；爬
	They are trying to climb the mountain. 他們試圖攀爬這座山。
hike	徒步旅行；健行
	Many people enjoy hiking in the forest. 許多人都喜歡在森林裡健行。
walk through	漫步
	Many people enjoy walking through the forest.
	許多人都喜歡在森林裡漫步。
sail on	航行
	Several boats are sailing on the ocean. 好幾艘船正在海上航行。

Word Families ⊙ 023

beach	海灘
	Many beaches by seas have sand. 在海邊的海灘多數都會有沙。
coast	海岸
	The American coast is thousands of miles long. 美國海岸長好幾千哩。
riverbank	河岸
	The shore of a river is called the riverbank. 河的岸邊稱為河岸。

land 土地

water 水源

gas 天然氣

Natural Resources 自然資源

air 空氣

oil 石油

tree 樹木

Checkup

A

Write | 請依提示寫出正確的英文單字。

1	江；河	_____	9	海洋	_____
2	湖泊	_____	10	島；島嶼	_____
3	小河	_____	11	圍繞著……	_____
4	森林	_____	12	由……組成	_____
5	草原	_____	13	攀登；爬	_____
6	沙漠	_____	14	漫步	_____
7	山	_____	15	航行	_____
8	丘陵	_____	16	海岸	_____

B

Complete the Sentences | 請在空格中填入最適當的答案，並視情況做適當的變化。

river	island	ocean	stream	hill
desert	mountain	beach	lake	forest

1 Most _____ flow to a sea or an ocean. 大部分的河都流向海洋。

2 Most _____ are hot and sandy and get very little rain.
大部分的沙漠既熱且多沙，降雨稀少。

3 An _____ is a very large body of salt water. 海洋是一大片的鹹水。

4 Mount Everest is the highest _____ in the world.
聖母峰是世界上最高的山。

5 A _____ is a large body of water surrounded by land.
湖是由大量的水組成，四周環繞著陸地。

6 A _____ is a small, narrow river. 溪流是一條又小又狹窄的河流。

7 _____ are not as high as mountains. 丘陵不如山高。

8 Many _____ by seas have sand. 在海邊的海灘多數都會有沙。

C

Read and Choose | 閱讀下列句子，並且選出最適當的答案。

1 An island is (surrounded by | made up of) water.

2 Many people enjoy (climbing | hiking) in the forest.

3 Several boats are (sailing | flowing) on the ocean.

4 The earth is (made up from | made up of) land and water.

Look, Read, and Write | 看圖並且依照提示，在空格中填入正確答案。

 1 ▸ a large body of water surrounded by land

_____

 4 ▸ a very large body of salt water

_____

 2 ▸ a large, steel hill

_____

 5 ▸ It has many kinds of trees.

_____

 3 ▸ a body of land surrounded by water

_____

 6 ▸ It is hot and sandy and gets little rain.

_____

 E

Read and Answer | 閱讀並且回答下列問題。 024

National Parks

The United States has many national parks. These are protected areas. So people cannot develop or damage them.

The first national park was Yellowstone National Park. It is an area with stunning scenery and many wild animals. The Grand Canyon is also a national park. It is one of the largest canyons in the world. Every year, millions of people visit these parks. They tour the parks and go hiking. Some even camp in the parks. They learn about the land and how to preserve it, too.

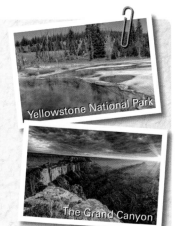

Yellowstone National Park

The Grand Canyon

Answer the questions.

1 What country has many national parks? _____

2 What was the first national park? _____

3 What is one of the world's largest canyons? _____

4 What do people do at national parks?

Key Words

🎧 025

01 **Asia**
[ˋeʃə]

(n.) 亞洲　　*Asian 亞洲的；亞洲人

Asia is the largest continent on Earth. 亞洲是世界上面積最廣大的大陸。

02 **Europe**
[ˋjʊrəp]

(n.) 歐洲　　*European 歐洲的；歐洲人

Countries like England, Germany, and Italy are in Europe.
英國、德國和義大利等國家都位於歐洲。

03 **Australia**
[ɔˋstreljə]

(n.) 澳洲　　*Australian 澳洲的；澳洲人

Australia is in the Southern Hemisphere. 澳洲位於南半球。

04 **North America**
[nɔrθ əˋmɛrɪkə]

(n.) 北美洲

The United States is located in North America. 美國位於北美洲。

05 **South America**
[saʊθ əˋmɛrɪkə]

(n.) 南美洲

The Amazon River flows through South America.
亞馬遜河流經南美洲。

06 **Africa**
[ˋæfrɪkə]

(n.) 非洲　　*African 非洲的；非洲人

Lions, tigers, and elephants are all animals living in Africa.
獅子、老虎和大象都是棲息於非洲的動物。

07 **Antarctica**
[ænˋtɑrktɪkə]

(n.) 南極洲

Antarctica is the coldest continent. 南極洲是最寒冷的一洲。

08 **Pacific Ocean**
[pəˋsɪfɪk ˋoʃən]

(n.) 太平洋

The Pacific Ocean is larger than every other ocean.
太平洋的面積比其他的海洋都還廣大。

09 **Atlantic Ocean**
[ətˋlæntɪk ˋoʃən]

(n.) 大西洋

The Atlantic Ocean is between Europe and the Americas.
大西洋位於歐洲和美洲之間。

10 **Indian Ocean**
[ˋɪndɪən ˋoʃən]

(n.) 印度洋

The Indian Ocean lies south of India and east of Africa.
印度洋位於印度的南方和非洲的東邊。

Oceans and Continents

be next to	緊鄰著 Turkey is next to Greece. 土耳其緊鄰著希臘。
adjoin [əˈdʒɔɪn]	毗連；毗鄰著 Turkey adjoins Greece. 土耳其毗鄰著希臘。
be located in	位於 Korea is located in eastern Asia. 韓國位於東亞。
be situated in [ˈsɪtʃu͵etɪd]	位於 Korea is situated in eastern Asia. 韓國位於東亞。
lie in	位於；置於；呈……狀態 Korea lies in eastern Asia. 韓國位於東亞。

island	島；島嶼 The island is located in the middle of the ocean. 這座島位於海洋的中間。
peninsula [pəˈnɪnsələ]	半島 A peninsula is surrounded by water on three sides. 半島三面皆環海。
land	陸地 Any area that is not covered by water is called land. 沒有被水覆蓋的地方稱為陸地。
continent	大陸 The world has seven continents. 世界有七大洲。

sea	海；海洋 The Mediterranean Sea separates Europe from Africa. 地中海將歐洲和非洲劃分開來。
ocean	海洋 The world has five oceans. 世界有五大海洋。
bay	（湖泊或海的）灣 A bay is an ocean area near land that is smaller than a gulf. 灣是指靠近陸地的海洋區域，面積較海灣小。
gulf	海灣 The Gulf of Mexico is located between Mexico and the United States. 墨西哥灣座落在墨西哥和美國之間。

Checkup

A Write | 請依提示寫出正確的英文單字。

1	亞洲	_____	
2	歐洲	_____	
3	非洲	_____	
4	澳洲	_____	
5	北美洲	_____	
6	南美洲	_____	
7	南極洲	_____	
8	太平洋	_____	

9	大西洋	_____
10	印度洋	_____
11	緊鄰著	_____
12	位於	_____
13	陸地	_____
14	（湖泊或海的）灣	_____
15	海灣	_____
16	半島	_____

B Complete the Sentences | 請在空格中填入最適當的答案，並視情況做適當的變化。

ocean	South America	bay	Europe	Africa
located	Pacific Ocean	Asia	continent	land

1 _____ is the largest continent on Earth. 亞洲是世界上面積最廣大的大陸。

2 Countries like England, Germany, and Italy are in _____.
英國、德國和義大利等國家都位於歐洲。

3 The Amazon River flows through _____ _____.
亞馬遜河流經南美洲。

4 Korea is _____ in eastern Asia. 韓國位於東亞。

5 Lions, tigers, and elephants are all animals living in _____.
獅子、老虎和大象都是棲息於非洲的動物。

6 Any area that is not covered by water is called _____.
沒有被水覆蓋的地方稱為陸地。

7 The _____ _____ is larger than every other ocean.
太平洋的面積比其他的海洋都還廣大。

8 The world has seven _____. 世界有七大洲。

C Read and Choose | 閱讀下列句子，並且選出最適當的答案。

1 The United States is located in (North America | South America).

2 A peninsula is surrounded by (land | water) on three sides.

3 Turkey (is next to | lies in) Greece.

4 The island is located in the middle of the (land | ocean).

Look, Read, and Write | 看圖並且依照提示，在空格中填入正確答案。

1  ▸ a piece of land
surrounded by water
_____

4  ▸ the largest ocean in
the world
_____

2  ▸ the largest continent
on Earth
_____

5  ▸ the ocean between
Europe and the
Americas
_____

3 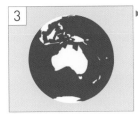 ▸ the continent that
is in the Southern
Hemisphere
_____

6  ▸ the ocean south of
India and east of
Africa
_____

 E

Read and Answer | 閱讀並且回答下列問題。 028

Oceans and Continents

There are seven continents on Earth. Asia is the
biggest of all of them. Europe has many countries
located in it. Africa has both deserts and jungles in
it. Asia, Europe, and Africa are often called "the Old
World." Australia is the largest island on Earth. People call North and South
America "the New World."

There are five oceans on Earth. The Pacific is the biggest. The Atlantic lies
between the Old World and the New World. The Indian Ocean is the only
ocean named for a country. The Arctic and Antarctic oceans are both very cold.

What is NOT true?

1   Asia is part of the Old World.

2   Australia is a big island.

3   The earth has seven oceans on it.

4   The Pacific Ocean is bigger than the Arctic Ocean.

Key Words 029

01 **map**
[mæp]

(n.) 地圖　*on the map 出名的　*off the map 不易找到的

Maps show people the locations of places.
地圖指出很多地點的位置。

02 **symbol**
[ˈsɪmb!]

(n.) 符號；象徵　*national symbol 國家象徵

A symbol is a picture that stands for a real thing on a map.
符號是一種圖像，在地圖中代表實際的事物。

03 **map key**
[mæp ki]

(n.) 地標　*map out 安排

The map key explains what the symbols on a map mean.
地標對地圖中的符號加以說明。

04 **compass**
[ˈkʌmpəs]

(n.) 羅盤；指南針；界線　*magnetic compass 磁羅盤

A compass shows what direction you're going.
指南針顯示了你正要前往的方向。

05 **location**
[loˈkeʃən]

(n.) 位置；場所；所在地　*on location 在外景拍攝的

We find the locations of places on maps.
我們找到了很多地點在地圖的位置了。

06 **direction**
[dəˈrɛkʃən]

(n.) 方向；指導　*sense of direction 方向感

North, south, east, and west are the four main directions.
北方、南方、東方和西方是四個主要方位。

07 **route**
[rut]

(n.) 路線；航線；途徑　*escape route 逃生路線

Take a route to go from one place to another.
採取一條從某地方到另一個地方的路線。

08 **instructions**
[ɪnˈstrʌknəns]

(n.)〔複〕指示；命令　*instruction manual 說明書

Follow instructions to get to your destination.
依照指示你就能夠到達目的地。

09 **turn**
[tɝn]

(v.) 轉向；翻轉 *(n.)* 轉動；轉向　*turn one's back on sb. 對某人置之不理

Turn right at the intersection. 在十字路口右轉。

10 **intersection**
[ˌɪntəˈsɛʃən]

(n.) 十字路口；交叉點；交叉　*busy intersection 繁忙的十字路口

An intersection is where two roads meet. 十字路口就是兩條路相交的地方。

map　symbol

Map Key
School
Gas Station

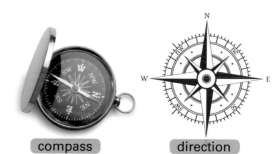

compass　direction

mean	表示……的意思；意指
	Blue means water on a map. 藍色在地圖中表示水。
symbolize	象徵；用符號表示
[ˈsɪmbḷˌaɪz]	Blue symbolizes water on a map. 藍色在地圖中象徵水。
stand for	代表；象徵
	Blue stands for water on a map. 藍色在地圖中代表水。
be located	位於……
	The bank is located next to the supermarket. 銀行位於超市隔壁。
get lost	迷失；迷路
	Maps keep people from getting lost. 地圖讓人們免於迷路。
become lost	迷失；迷路
	Maps keep people from becoming lost. 地圖讓人們免於迷路。
take	採取；接受
	They are taking the fastest route. 他們走最快的一條路線。
follow	採用；沿著……行進
	They are following the fastest route. 他們沿著一條最快的路線行進。

Word Families ⊙ 031

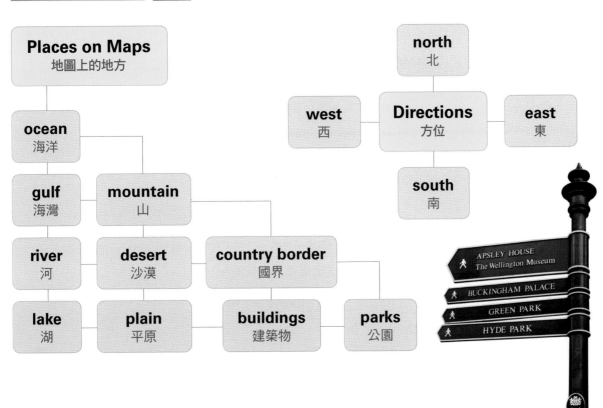

Places on Maps
地圖上的地方

ocean
海洋

gulf
海灣

mountain
山

river
河

desert
沙漠

country border
國界

lake
湖

plain
平原

buildings
建築物

parks
公園

north
北

west
西

Directions
方位

east
東

south
南

Checkup

A

Write | 請依提示寫出正確的英文單字。

1	地圖	_____	9	路線；航線	_____
2	符號	_____	10	指示；命令	_____
3	地標	_____	11	表示……的意思	_____
4	指南針	_____	12	象徵；用符號表示	_____
5	位置	_____	13	西	_____
6	方向	_____	14	位於……	_____
7	十字路口	_____	15	迷失；迷路	_____
8	轉向	_____	16	採取；接受	_____

B

Complete the Sentences | 請在空格中填入最適當的答案，並視情況做適當的變化。

compass	mean	stand for	route	symbol
instructions	turn	location	north	follow

1 Maps show people the _____ of places. 地圖指出很多地點的位置。

2 A symbol is a picture that _____ _____ a real thing on a map.
符號是一種圖像，在地圖中代表實際的事物。

3 The map key explains what the _____ on a map mean.
地標對地圖中的符號加以說明。

4 Take a _____ to go from one place to another.
採取一條從某地方到另一個地方的路線。

5 Follow _____ to get to your destination. 依照指示你就能夠到達目的地。

6 _____ right at the intersection. 在十字路口右轉。

7 _____, south, east, and west are the four main directions.
北方、南方、東方和西方是四個主要方位。

8 They are _____ the fastest route. 他們沿著一條最快的路線行進。

C

Read and Choose | 閱讀下列句子，並且選出最適當的答案。

1 Maps keep people from (getting lost | taking a route).

2 They are (taking | getting) the fastest route.

3 The bank is (located | turned) next to the supermarket.

4 Blue (follows | stands for) water on a map.

D Look, Read, and Write | 看圖並且依照提示，在空格中填入正確答案。

 ▶ It shows the locations of places.

_____

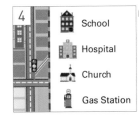 ▶ It explains what the symbols on a map mean.

School
Hospital
Church
Gas Station

_____

 ▶ the choice of roads taken to get to a place

_____

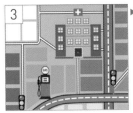 ▶ a place where two roads meet

_____

 ▶ a picture that stands for a real thing on a map

_____

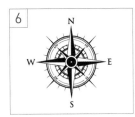 ▶ North, south, east, and west are the four main _____.

E Read and Answer | 閱讀並且回答下列問題。 🔊 032

What Is a Map?

Maps are drawings of different places. They show what an area looks like. Some maps show very large areas, like countries. Other maps show small areas, like cities or neighborhoods.

Maps can show many things. On big maps, they show the land and water. These maps have countries, seas, oceans, and even continents on them. People use these maps to find countries and cities. Small maps might show one city or area. They have many details. They have individual buildings and streets on them. People use these maps to find their way somewhere.

Fill in the blanks.

1   _____ show what an area looks like.
2   Maps can show small areas, like _____ or neighborhoods.
3   Big maps have countries, _____, oceans, and continents.
4   Small maps have individual _____ and streets on them.

Unit 09 Our Earth and Its Resources

Key Words
🔊 033

01 natural resources
[ˈnætʃərəl rɪˈsorsɪz]
(n.) 自然資源　*commodities 原物料
Oil, coal, and gas are **natural resources**. 石油、煤礦和瓦斯都是自然資源。

02 endangered
[ɪnˈdendʒəd]
(a.) 快要絕種的　*endangered species 瀕臨絕種的動植物
Tigers and pandas are **endangered** animals.
老虎和熊貓都是瀕臨絕種的動物。

03 extinct
[ɪkˈstɪŋkt]
(a.) 絕種的；熄滅了的；廢除了的；過時的　*extinct volcano 死火山
Extinct species are no longer alive. 絕種的動物已不存在。

04 recycling bin
[ˌriˈsaɪklɪŋ bɪn]
(n.) 資源回收桶 = recycle bin
We can put paper and glass in the **recycling bin**.
我們可以把紙類和玻璃放入資源回收桶。

05 environment
[ɪnˈvaɪrənmənt]
(n.) 環境；自然環境　*surroundings 環境；周圍的情況
It's important to keep the **environment** clean.
維護環境整潔是很重要的事情。

06 pollution
[pəˈluʃən]
(n.) 污染；污染物；污染地區　*air pollution 空氣汙染
Air and water **pollution** are very harmful. 空氣和水污染造成很大的危害。

07 dirty
[ˈdɝtɪ]
(a.) 髒的；卑鄙的　*dirty work 詐騙；不法行為
Pollution makes the earth **dirty**. 污染使地球髒亂。

08 trash can
[træʃ kæn]
(n.) 垃圾桶 = garbage can
Everyone should throw garbage in the **trash can**.
每個人都應該把垃圾丟入垃圾桶裡。

09 responsibility
[rɪˌspɑnsəˈbɪlətɪ]
(n.) 責任；職責　*be proud of 為……感到驕傲
It's everyone's **responsibility** to take care of the environment.
維護環境是每個人的職責。

10 conservation
[ˌkɑnsəˈveʃən]
(n.) 保存；保護；管理　*take responsibility for 對……（事情）責任
Conservation can save natural resources. 資源保育可以拯救自然資源。

sign of recycling

environmental poster
GO GREEN

GO ORGANIC GO NATURAL for healthy life
SAVE THE PLANET
conservation motto

recycle
回收
We can **recycle** items like cans, bottles, and newspapers.
我們可以把紙類和玻璃放入資源回收筒。

reuse
重複利用
Try to **reuse** paper and boxes more than one time.
要試著多次重複利用紙張和盒子。

preserve
[prɪˋzɝv]
保護；維護
We need to **preserve** the environment. 我們必須保護環境。

save
維護；節約；拯救
We need to **save** the environment. 我們必須維護環境。

take care of
照顧
We need to **take care of** the environment. 我們必須照顧環境。

waste
[west]
浪費；消耗；濫用
Do not **waste** our valuable natural resources. 不要浪費我們珍貴的自然資源。

care for
照料；照顧
Some people really **care for** endangered animals.
有的人很照顧瀕臨絕種的動物。

care about
關心；在乎；介意
Some people really **care about** endangered animals.
有的人很關心瀕臨絕種的動物。

Word Families 🔊 035

paper 紙張
glass 玻璃
water 水
minerals 礦物

cans 鋁罐
Items to Recycle 可回收物品
Natural Resources 自然資源
oil 石油

metal 金屬
plastic 塑膠
coal 煤礦
gas 天然氣

PAPER
PLASTIC
GLASS

Checkup

A

Write | 請依提示寫出正確的英文單字。

1	自然資源	_____	9	快要絕種的	_____
2	絕種的	_____	10	保存;保護	_____
3	資源回收桶	_____	11	關心;在乎	_____
4	環境	_____	12	回收	_____
5	責任;職責	_____	13	重複利用	_____
6	污染	_____	14	節約;拯救	_____
7	髒的	_____	15	浪費;消耗	_____
8	垃圾桶	_____	16	照顧	_____

B

Complete the Sentences | 請在空格中填入最適當的答案,並視情況做適當的變化。

extinct	endangered	environment	natural resources
conservation	pollution	responsibility	recycling bin

1 Oil, coal, and gas are _____ _____. 石油、煤礦和瓦斯都是自然資源。

2 Tigers and pandas are _____ animals. 老虎和熊貓都是瀕臨絕種的動物。

3 We can put paper and glass in the _____ _____.
我們可以把紙類和玻璃放入資源回收桶。

4 Air and water _____ are very harmful. 空氣和水污染造成很大的危害。

5 It's important to keep the _____ clean. 維護環境整潔是很重要的事情。

6 _____ species are no longer alive. 絕種的動物已不存在。

7 It's everyone's _____ to take care of the environment.
照顧環境是每個人的職責。

8 _____ can save natural resources. 資源保育可以拯救自然資源。

C

Read and Choose | 請選出與鋪底字意思相近的答案。

1 We can recycle items like cans, bottles, and newspapers.

   a. waste   b. reuse   c. care for

2 We need to preserve the environment.

   a. save   b. reuse   c. recycle

3 Some people really care for endangered animals.

   a. save   b. keep   c. care about

Look, Read, and Write | 看圖並且依照提示，在空格中填入正確答案。

There are four recycling bins.

Put each item into the proper bin and write the bin's number.

1	2	3	4

▶ _____ ▶ _____ ▶ _____ ▶ _____

❶  PAPER ❷  METALS ❸  PLASTIC ❹  GLASS

E

Read and Answer | 閱讀並且回答下列問題。 🔊 036

Endangered Animals

There are many animals on the earth. Some species have many animals. But there are just a few animals in other species. These animals are endangered. If we aren't careful, they could all die and become extinct. In China, the panda is endangered. In the oceans, the blue whale is endangered. In Africa, lions, tigers, and elephants are all endangered. There are many other endangered animals, too. What can people do? People can stop hunting them. And people can set aside land for the animals to live on. Then, maybe one day, they will not be endangered anymore.

What is true? Write T (true) or F (false).

1 All animals are endangered. _____

2 Some animals could all die and become extinct. _____

3 The panda is not endangered. _____

4 People should stop hunting endangered animals. _____

01 **Native American**
[`netɪv ə`mɛrɪkən]

(n.) 美洲印地安人

Native Americans were the first people who lived in America.
印地安人是最先居住在美洲的人類。

02 **tribe**
[traɪb]

(n.) 部落；種族　*kin group 親屬團體

Many American Indian tribes lived in America.
印地安部落多數都居住在美洲。

03 **New World**
[nju wɜld]

(n.) 新世界（指西半球或南、北美洲及其附近島嶼）

North and South America were called the New World.
北美洲和南美洲曾被稱為新世界。

04 **voyage**
[`vɔɪɪdʒ]

(n.) 航海；航空；航行；旅行　*bon voyage【法】一路平安

The voyage from Europe to the New World took many weeks.
從歐洲航行至新世界需要花上好幾個星期。

05 **explorer**
[ɪk`splorɚ]

(n.) 探險家；勘探者　*adventurer 冒險者

Christopher Columbus was the explorer who discovered America.
哥倫布是發現美洲大陸的探險家。

06 **treasure**
[`trɛʒɚ]

(n.) 寶藏；金銀財寶 *(v.)* 珍愛　*treasure hunt 尋寶遊戲

The Spanish were looking for treasure in the New World.
西班牙人在新世界尋找寶藏。

07 ***Mayflower***
[`me,flauɚ]

(n.) 五月花號

The Pilgrims sailed on a ship called the *Mayflower*.
英國清教徒乘坐著一艘叫作五月花號的船。

08 **freedom**
[`fridəm]

(n.) 自由　*freedom of speech 言論自由 *freedom fighter 自由鬥士

The Pilgrims came to America for religious freedom.
英國清教徒為了宗教自由而前往美國。

09 **war**
[wɔr]

(n.) 戰爭；鬥爭　*warlike 好戰的；尚武的

Native Americans and Europeans fought many wars.
美洲印地安人和歐洲人之間曾發生多次鬥爭。

10 **colony**
[`kɑlənɪ]

(n.) 殖民地；僑居地；聚居地；聚居人群　*British colony 英屬殖民地

The English started several colonies in North America.
英國人開始在北美洲各處設立殖民地。

Columbus's arrival in the New World

Native Americans

Mayflower and the Pilgrims

Pilgrims praying

discover

發現；發覺

Christopher Columbus **discovered** North America in 1492.
哥倫布於 1492 年發現了北美洲。

explore

探測；探勘；探索

Many Spanish **explored** all around the New World.
許多西班牙人都在新世界進行探勘活動。

land

登陸；降落

The Pilgrims **landed** in America at Plymouth Rock in 1620.
英國清教徒於 1620 年登陸在美國的普利茅斯石（移民石）。

colonize
[ˈkɑlənaɪz]

開拓殖民地；移居於殖民地

The English **colonized** parts of America.
英國人將美國的一些地方開拓為殖民地。

settle in

使定居；殖民於

The English **settled in** parts of America. 英國人定居於美國的部分地區。

be different from 和⋯⋯不同

The Native Americans' way of life **was** very **different from** that of the explorers.
美洲印地安人的生活方式，與那些探險家的十分不同。

Pilgrim
[ˈpɪlgrɪm]

英國清教徒（1620年搭乘五月花號移居美國的英國清教徒）
The **Pilgrims** wanted religious freedom. 英國清教徒想要有宗教自由。

Puritan
[ˈpjurətən]

清教徒
The **Puritans** settled in Massachusetts. 清教徒定居於麻薩諸塞州。

Early American Empires
美洲古帝國

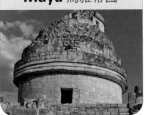

Maya 馬雅帝國

Aztec 阿茲特克帝國

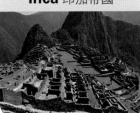

Inca 印加帝國

European Explorers
歐洲探險家

Christopher Columbus
哥倫布

Hernando Cortez
科爾特斯

Ponce De Leon
龐塞・德萊昂

Sir Walter Raleigh
羅利

John Smith
約翰・史密斯

Checkup

A

Write | 請依提示寫出正確的英文單字。

1	美洲印地安人	_____	9	五月花號	_____
2	部落；種族	_____	10	發現；發覺	_____
3	新世界	_____	11	探測；探勘	_____
4	航海；航行	_____	12	登陸；降落	_____
5	探險家	_____	13	開拓殖民地	_____
6	寶藏	_____	14	使定居	_____
7	自由	_____	15	英國清教徒	_____
8	殖民地	_____	16	清教徒	_____

B

Complete the Sentences | 請在空格中填入最適當的答案，並視情況做適當的變化。

war	Native American	explorer	voyage	*Mayflower*
land	New World	treasure	tribe	different

1 _____ _____ were the first people who lived in America.
印地安人是最先居住在美洲的人類。

2 The Pilgrims sailed on a ship called the _____.
英國清教徒乘坐著一艘叫作五月花號的船。

3 Christopher Columbus was the _____ who discovered America.
哥倫布是發現美洲大陸的探險家。

4 The _____ from Europe to the New World took many weeks.
從歐洲航行至新世界需要花上好幾個星期。

5 The Spanish were looking for _____ in the New World.
西班牙人在新世界尋找寶藏。

6 North and South America were called the _____ _____.
北美洲和南美洲曾被稱為新世界。

7 Many American Indian _____ lived in America. 印地安部落多數都居住在美洲。

8 The Native Americans' way of life was very _____ from that of the explorers.
美洲印地安人的生活方式，與那些探險家的十分不同。

C

Read and Choose | 閱讀下列句子，並且選出最適當的答案。

1 The (Pilgrims | explorers) wanted religious freedom.

2 The (English | Spanish) explored all around the New World.

3 The (Puritans | Spanish) settled in Massachusetts.

4 The English (colonized | sailed) parts of America.

D Look, Read, and Write | 看圖並且依照提示，在空格中填入正確答案。

 ▸ the first people who lived in America

_____

 ▸ the settlers who landed in America at Plymouth Rock

_____

 ▸ the ship the Pilgrims sailed on to come to North America

_____

 ▸ a country that is controlled by another country

_____

 ▸ a name used to refer to North and South America

_____

 ▸ Some early American empires were the Maya, Aztec, and

_____ .

E Read and Answer | 閱讀並且回答下列問題。 🔊 040

The Spanish in the New World

Christopher Columbus discovered the New World in 1492. After him, many Europeans began to visit the land. Most of the early explorers came from Spain. The Spanish wanted to get rich. So they looked for gold and silver. They were often very cruel to the natives.

They made war on them. So the Spanish killed many natives. They defeated the Aztecs. And they also defeated the Incas. They made many natives their slaves. They were not interested in being friends with them. They just wanted treasure.

Aztec emperor

Hernando Cortez

Answer the questions.

1   Who discovered the New World?

_____

2   What did the Spanish explorers want?

_____

3   What Native Americans did the Spanish defeat?

_____

4   What did the Spanish do to the defeated Native Americans?

_____

Review Test 2

A Write | 請依提示寫出正確的英文單字。

1 江；河	_____	11 圍繞著…… _____
2 湖泊	_____	12 由……組成 _____
3 太平洋	_____	13 緊鄰著 _____
4 半島	_____	14 位於 _____
5 地圖	_____	15 意指 _____
6 符號；象徵	_____	16 回收 _____
7 地標	_____	17 保護；維護 p_____
8 自然資源	_____	18 發現；發覺 _____
9 絕種的	_____	19 探測；探勘 _____
10 美洲印地安人	_____	20 登陸；降落 _____

B Choose the Correct Word | 請選出與鋪底字意思相近的答案。

1 Korea is located in eastern Asia.

   a. situated   b. made   c. next

2 We can recycle items like cans, bottles, and newspapers.

   a. waste   b. reuse   c. care for

3 We need to preserve the environment.

   a. save   b. reuse   c. recycle

4 Some people really care for endangered animals.

   a. save   b. keep   c. care about

C Complete the Sentences | 請在空格中填入最適當的答案，並視情況做適當的變化。

Native American	Asia	ocean	location

1 An _____ is a very large body of salt water. 海洋充滿了大量鹹水。

2 _____ is the largest continent on Earth. 亞洲是世界上面積最廣大的大陸。

3 Maps show people the _____ of places. 地圖指出很多地點的位置。

4 _____ _____ were the first people who lived in America.
印地安人是最先居住在美洲的人類。

52

CHAPTER 3

Science ①

Unit 11 Seasons and Weather 季節和氣候

Key Words 🔊 041

01	**season** ['sizn]	(n.) 季節 　*season (v.) 給……調味 The weather changes with each **season**. 天氣隨著每個季節而變換。
02	**spring** [sprɪŋ]	(n.) 春天 　*spring 源泉 　*spring up 湧現 In **spring**, the flowers begin to bloom. 花兒在春天開始綻放。
03	**summer** ['sʌmɚ]	(n.) 夏天 　*high summer 盛夏 　*summer camp 夏令營 The weather is usually hot and sunny in **summer**. 夏天的天氣通常都是晴朗炎熱的。
04	**fall** [fɔl]	(n.) 秋天 = autumn The leaves change colors during **fall**. 葉子的顏色在秋天會改變。
05	**winter** ['wɪntɚ]	(n.) 冬天 　*wintertime 冬季 **Winter** is a time of cold weather and snow. 冬天是指寒冷天氣和下雪的時間。
06	**weather** ['wɛðɚ]	(n.) 天氣 　*climate 氣候 Rain, snow, and storms are all kinds of **weather**. 下雨、下雪和暴風雨都屬於天氣的種類。
07	**temperature** ['tɛmprətʃɚ]	(n.) 溫度；體溫 　*body temperature 體溫 The **temperature** is hot in summer and cold in winter. 夏天的溫度很炎熱，而冬天很寒冷。
08	**sunny** ['sʌnɪ]	(a.) 晴朗的；陽光充足的 　*sun (n.) 太陽 The weather is often **sunny** during summer. 夏天的天氣通常都是陽光普照。
09	**rainy** ['renɪ]	(a.) 下雨的；多雨的 　*rain (n.) 雨 In some places, it is very **rainy** in spring. 在某些地方，春天時常下雨。
10	**snowy** [snoɪ]	(a.) 下雪的；多雪的；雪白的 　*snow (n.) 雪 In some places, it is very **snowy** in winter. 在某些地方，冬天時常下雪。

Four Seasons

spring

summer

fall

winter

increase 增加
The temperature increases throughout the day. 白天的氣溫會持續上升。

get hotter | get warmer 變熱｜變溫暖
The temperature gets hotter throughout the day. 白天的氣溫會持續變熱。

decrease 減少
The temperature always decreases at night. 晚上的氣溫通常都會下降。

get colder | get cooler 變冷｜變涼
The temperature always gets colder at night. 晚上的氣溫通常都會變冷。

rain 下雨
It rains a lot in some parts of the country. 這個國家的某些地區時常下雨。

snow 下雪
Winter is the season when it usually snows. 冬天是時常下雪的季節。

fall 落下；降落
Snow falls in the winter. 冬天會降雪。

blow 吹；刮
The wind is blowing hard. 風吹得很強勁。

Word Families ⊙ 043

lightning 閃電
Lightning struck the tree during the storm. 在一場暴風雨中閃電擊中了這棵樹木。

thunder 雷聲；打雷
The thunder was incredibly loud. 雷聲大作。

sunny 晴朗的
rainy 下雨的
storm 暴風雨
typhoon 颱風
foggy 多霧的
Weather 天氣
snowy 下雪的
tornado 龍捲風
hurricane 颶風
cloudy 多雲的；陰天的
windy 刮風的

Checkup

A Write | 請依提示寫出正確的英文單字。

1	季節	_____	9	增加	_____
2	春天	_____	10	減少	_____
3	夏天	_____	11	下雨	_____
4	秋天；落下	_____	12	下雪	_____
5	冬天	_____	13	龍捲風	_____
6	天氣	_____	14	閃電	_____
7	溫度	_____	15	打雷	_____
8	吹；刮	_____	16	暴風雨	_____

B Complete the Sentences | 請在空格中填入最適當的答案，並視情況做適當的變化。

summer	spring	storm	temperature	fall
winter	rainy	snowy	weather	season

1 In _____, the flowers begin to bloom. 花兒在春天開始綻放。

2 The _____ is hot in summer. 夏天的溫度很炎熱。

3 The weather changes with each _____. 每個季節的天氣都會變換。

4 The leaves change colors during _____. 葉子的顏色在秋天會改變。

5 In some places, it is very _____ in spring. 在某些地方，春天時常下雨。

6 In some places, it is very _____ in winter. 在某些地方，冬天時常下雪。

7 The weather is usually hot and sunny in _____.
夏天的天氣通常都是陽光普照。

8 Snow falls in the _____. 冬天會降雪。

C Read and Choose | 閱讀下列句子，並且選出最適當的答案。

1 Rain, snow, and storms are all kinds of (seasons | weather).

2 The temperature (gets colder | gets warmer) at night.

3 The temperature (increases | decreases) throughout the day.

4 Winter is the season when it usually (rains | snows).

D Look, Read, and Write I 看圖並且依照提示，在空格中填入正確答案。

 ▸ having a lot of rain

_____

 ▸ snowing

_____

 ▸ full of light from the sun

_____

 ▸ very bright flashes of light in the sky

_____

 ▸ a loud noise coming from the sky

_____

 ▸ a measurement of how hot or how cold a place is

_____

E Read and Answer I 閱讀並且回答下列問題。 🔊 044

Seasons and Weather

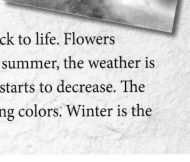

There are four seasons in a year. They are spring, summer, fall, and winter. Sometimes people say "autumn" instead of fall. Each season has different kinds of weather. In spring, the air gets warmer, and the weather is often rainy. Everything comes back to life. Flowers start to bloom, and leaves start growing on trees. In summer, the weather is usually very hot and sunny. In fall, the temperature starts to decrease. The weather gets cooler. The leaves on trees start changing colors. Winter is the coldest season. It usually snows during the winter.

What is true? Write T (true) or F (false).

1   Another word for fall is "autumn."   _____

2   The flowers begin blooming in summer.   _____

3   The weather is hotter in fall than in summer.   _____

4   It might snow during the winter.   _____

Key Words

🔊 045

01	**plant** [plænt]	*(n.)* 植物 *potted plant 盆栽 *power plant 發電廠 **Plants** need sunlight, air, water, and nutrients to grow. 植物需要陽光、空氣、水分和養分才能夠生長。
02	**leaf** [lif]	*(n.)* 葉；葉子 *leaves（複） **Leaves** use sunlight to make food for plants. 葉子利用陽光滋養植物。
03	**stem** [stɛm]	*(n.)* 莖；（樹）幹；柄；桿；血統 *stemmed 去掉莖（或梗）的 **Stems** carry water and nutrients from the roots to the leaves. 莖把水分和養分從根部運送到葉子。
04	**root** [rut]	*(n.)* 根；根源 *take root（種子）長出根來 *be rooted in 深植於 **Roots** absorb water and nutrients from the soil. 根會從土壤中吸收水分和養分。
05	**flower** ['flaʊɚ]	*(n.)* 花 *flower arranging 插花藝術 A part of the **flower** makes seeds. 花朵的某個部位會結實。
06	**soil** [sɔɪl]	*(n.)* 土壤 *dry soil 旱地 Good **soil** is necessary for plants to grow in. 肥沃的土壤對植物的生長是不可或缺的。
07	**nutrient** ['njutrɪənt]	*(n.)* 養分；營養物；滋養物 *essential nutrients 必需營養素 **Nutrients** let plants become strong and healthy. 養分讓植物變得健壯。
08	**sow** [so]	*(v.)* 播種 *self-sown 自然成長的 Farmers **sow** seeds in their fields. 農夫在田地裡播種。
09	**plant** [plænt]	*(v.)* 種植 *plant sth. out 移植（植物） We **plant** trees so that new ones will grow. 我們種樹是為了讓新的得以生長。
10	**water** ['wɔtɚ]	*(v.)* 澆水 *water down 稀釋 You must **water** plants regularly. 你必須按時澆水。

Parts of a Plant

flower

leaf

stem

fruit with seeds

grow	生長；成長
	A plant needs air, water, and sunlight to grow.
	植物需要空氣、水分和陽光才能夠生長。
get bigger	變大；長大
	A plant needs air, water, and sunlight to get bigger.
	植物需要空氣、水分和陽光才能夠長大。

bloom	開花；繁榮
	The flower is blooming right now. 那朵花現在正在綻放。
blossom [ˋblɑlsəm]	開花；生長茂盛
	The apple tree is blossoming right now. 那棵蘋果樹現在正在開花。

produce	生產；製作
	Many trees and plants produce fruit. 很多樹和植物都會產出果實。
bear	開（花）；結（果）；生（小孩）
	Many trees and plants bear fruit. 很多樹和植物都會結出果實。

absorb [əbˋsɔrb]	吸收（液體、氣、光等）
	Roots absorb water from the soil. 根會從土壤中吸收水分。
take in	接受；吸收
	Roots take in water from the soil. 根會從土壤中吸收水分。

Word Families ⊙ 047

branch

trunk

branch	枝；樹枝
	Branches connect to the stem and have leaves on them.
	與莖部相連的樹枝上都長有葉子。
trunk	樹幹
	Trunks are the thick main stems of trees. 粗厚的樹幹是樹木的主莖。

flower	花；花卉
	Some common flowers are roses, lilies, and daisies.
	玫瑰、百合花和雛菊是一些常見的花。
blossom	（果樹的）花
	Most trees have blossoms in the springtime. 大部分的樹都會在春天開花。

fruit	水果；果實
	Apples, oranges, and bananas are fruits that grow on trees.
	蘋果、柳橙和香蕉都是生長在樹上的水果。
vegetable	蔬菜
	Carrots, potatoes, and tomatoes are vegetables. 胡蘿蔔、馬鈴薯和番茄都是蔬菜。

Checkup

A

Write | 請依提示寫出正確的英文單字。

1	植物	_____	9	澆水 _____
2	葉	_____	10	開花；繁榮 _____
3	莖	_____	11	開花；生長茂盛 _____
4	根	_____	12	生長；成長 _____
5	花	_____	13	生產；製作 _____
6	土壤	_____	14	吸收 a_____
7	養分	_____	15	枝；樹枝 _____
8	種植	_____	16	水果；果實 _____

B

Complete the Sentences | 請在空格中填入最適當的答案，並視情況做適當的變化。

leaf	plant	flower	stem	nutrient
sow	sunlight	bloom	fruit	root

1 _____ need sunlight, air, and water to grow.
植物需要陽光、空氣、水分和養分才能夠生長。

2 A part of the _____ makes seeds. 花朵的某個部位會結實。

3 _____ carry water and nutrients from the roots. 莖會從根部取得水分和養分。

4 _____ use sunlight to make food. 葉子利用陽光製造養料。

5 _____ let plants become strong. 養分讓植物變得健壯。

6 The flower is _____ right now. 那朵花現在正在綻放。

7 Apples and bananas are _____ that grow on trees.
蘋果和香蕉都是生長在樹上的水果。

8 Farmers _____ seeds in their fields. 農夫在田地裡播種。

C

Read and Choose | 請選出與鋪底字意思相近的答案。

1 A plant needs air, water, and sunlight to grow.

a. get bigger   b. carry   c. absorb

2 Many trees and plants produce fruit.

a. sow   b. bear   c. water

3 Roots take in water from the soil.

a. carry   b. absorb   c. make food

Look, Read, and Write | 看圖並且依照提示，在空格中填入正確答案完成句子。

Which parts of a plant are they? Complete the sentences.

 1 ▶ _____ make food for plants.

 4 ▶ _____ make seeds for plants.

 2 ▶ _____ carry water to the leaves.

 5 ▶ _____ are the thick main stems of trees.

 3 ▶ _____ absorb water and nutrients from the soil.

 6 ▶ _____ is necessary for plants.

E

Read and Answer | 閱讀並且回答下列問題。 🔊 048

How Plants Grow

Let's grow some plants in a garden. First, we need some seeds. We have to plant the seeds in the soil, and then we should give them water. After a few days or weeks, the plants will start growing above the ground. First, they will be tiny, but they will become taller every day.

Now, the plants need plenty of sunlight, water, and nutrients in order to get bigger. Slowly, the stems will grow higher, and the plants will get branches and leaves. Some of them will start to blossom. These blossoms will turn into fruit we can eat later. A part of these blossoms makes seeds. They help plants make new plants.

What is true? Write T (true) or F (false).

1 Plants grow from seeds.   _____

2 Seeds do not need water.   _____

3 Plants only need water and nutrients.   _____

4 Blossoms often become fruit later.   _____

Key Words
🔊 049

01	**living thing** [ˈlɪvɪŋ ˈθɪŋ]	*(n.)* 生物 Animals and plants are living things. 動物和植物都是生物。
02	**habitat** [ˈhæbəˌtæt]	*(n.)*（動物）棲息地；（植物）產地　　*natural habitat 自然棲息地 A habitat is a place where animals and plants live. 棲息地是動物和植物生長的地方。
03	**forest** [ˈfɔrɪst]	*(n.)* 森林　　*forest park 森林公園 Squirrels, deer, and bears live in forest habitats. 松鼠、鹿和熊都居住在森林裡。
04	**underground** [ˈʌndəˌgraʊnd]	*(n.)* 地面下層 *(a.)* 地下的　　*underground railway 地下鐵道 Some underground animals are moles, gophers, and worms. 鼴鼠、地鼠和蟲都是居住在地底下的動物。
05	**desert** [ˈdɛzət]	*(n.)* 沙漠　　* 相似形字：dessert 甜點 The desert habitat is very hot and dry. 沙漠是一個又熱又乾燥的地方。
06	**water** [ˈwɔtə]	*(n.)* 水　　*by water 乘船　　*like water（花錢）無節制地；大量地 Fish, whales, and dolphins live in water habitats. 魚、鯨魚和海豚都住在水中。
07	**grassland** [ˈgræsˌlænd]	*(n.)* 草原；牧草地　　*wet grassland 草原溼地 Grasslands are flat areas with grass and no trees. 草原是長滿青草、沒有樹木的平地。
08	**environment** [ɪnˈvaɪrənmənt]	*(n.)* 環境；自然環境　　* natural environment 自然環境 A rainforest is a wet and hot environment. 雨林是一個溼熱的環境。
09	**life cycle** [laɪf ˈsaɪkḷ]	*(n.)* 生命週期　　*entire life cycle 整個生命週期 Every animal goes through a life cycle of birth, life, and death. 所有動物都會經過出生、生活與死亡的週期。
10	**live in** [lɪv ɪn]	*(v.)* 生活在；居住在　　*lived-in 家居的；飽經風霜的 Few animals live in the desert. 很少有動物住在沙漠裡。

Habitats

forest

desert

ocean

tundra

survive	活下來；倖存 Animals need food, water, and oxygen to survive. 動物需要食物、水和氧氣才能夠生存。
stay alive	活著 Animals need food, water, and oxygen to stay alive. 動物需要食物、水和氧氣才能夠活著。
adapt	適應 Animals and plants adapt to survive in their environment. 動物和植物為了生存而適應環境。
change	改變 Animals and plants change to survive in their environment. 動物和植物為了在環境中生存而改變。
die out	逐漸消失；滅絕 The dinosaurs died out millions of years ago. 恐龍數百萬年前就消失了。
become extinct	絕種；滅絕 The dinosaurs became extinct millions of years ago. 恐龍數百萬年前就絕種了。

Word Families 🔊 051

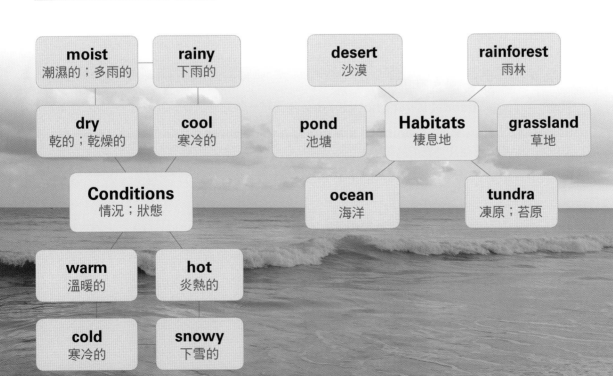

moist 潮濕的；多雨的

rainy 下雨的

desert 沙漠

rainforest 雨林

dry 乾的；乾燥的

cool 寒冷的

pond 池塘

Habitats 棲息地

grassland 草地

Conditions 情況；狀態

ocean 海洋

tundra 凍原；苔原

warm 溫暖的

hot 炎熱的

cold 寒冷的

snowy 下雪的

Checkup

Write | 請依提示寫出正確的英文單字。

1	棲息地	_____	9	生命週期	_____
2	生物	_____	10	活下來；倖存	_____
3	沙漠	_____	11	活著	_____
4	森林	_____	12	適應	_____
5	地下的	_____	13	改變	_____
6	草地	_____	14	逐漸消失	_____
7	環境	_____	15	潮濕的	_____
8	雨林	_____	16	生活在	_____

B

Complete the Sentences | 請在空格中填入最適當的答案，並視情況做適當的變化。

habitat	forest	underground	desert	living thing
life cycle	live in	rainforest	grassland	environment

1 Animals and plants are _____ _____. 動物和植物都是生物。

2 A _____ is a place where animals and plants live.
   棲息地是動物和植物生長的地方。

3 Every animal goes through a _____ _____ of birth, life, and death.
   所有動物都會經過出生、生活與死亡的週期。

4 Squirrels, deer, and bears live in _____ habitats.
   松鼠、鹿和熊都居住在森林裡。

5 A rainforest is a wet and hot _____. 雨林是一個溼熱的環境。

6 The _____ habitat is very hot and dry. 沙漠是一個又熱又乾燥的地方。

7 Some _____ animals are moles and gophers.
   鼴鼠和地鼠都是居住在地底下的動物。

8 Few animals _____ _____ the desert. 很少有動物住在沙漠裡。

C

Read and Choose | 請選出與鋪底字意思相近的答案。

1 Animals need food, water, and oxygen to stay alive.
   a. change   b. adapt   c. survive

2 Animals and plants adapt to survive in their environment.
   a. go through   b. change   c. live

3 The dinosaurs died out millions of years ago.
   a. lived in   b. became extinct c. hunted

Look, Read, and Write | 看圖並且依照提示，在空格中填入正確答案。

What are the habitats?

 1 ▸ a place where it is very hot and dry
_____

 4 ▸ a place where fish and whales live
_____

 2 ▸ a place where squirrels and bears live
_____

 5 ▸ flat areas with grass and no trees
_____

 3 ▸ a place where moles and worms live
_____

 6 ▸ a place where it is wet and hot
_____

E

Read and Answer | 閱讀並且回答下列問題。 052

Places to Live

An animal's habitat is very important. It has everything an animal needs to survive. Most animals can't live in other habitats. Fish live in the water. They can't survive in the desert. Deer live in the forest. They can't survive in the jungle.

What makes a habitat unique? There are many things. Two of them are more important than the others. They are weather and temperature. These two help certain plants grow. Many animals use these plants for food and shelter. Without them, the animals could not live in those habitats.

What is true? Write T (true) or F (false).

1   Habitats are not important to animals.   _____
2   Deer can live in the jungle.   _____
3   A habitat's weather is very important.   _____
4   Animals use plants to make shelter.   _____

Key Words 🔘 053

01	**ocean** [`oʃən]	(n.) 海洋　*be on the ocean 在海洋上 Can you name the world's five oceans? 你可以說出世界五大海洋的名字嗎？
02	**undersea** [`ʌndɚ`si]	(a.) 海底的；海裡的 (adv.) 在海底　*undersea volcano 海底火山 Many kinds of plants and animals live in the undersea world. 海底世界住了多種植物和動物。
03	**shore** [ʃor]	(n.) 岸　*on shore 在岸上 The shore is where the sea and land meet. 海岸就是大海與陸地相連的地方。
04	**tide** [taɪd]	(n.) 潮水；浪潮；潮流　*turn the tide 扭轉局勢　*at high tide 漲潮時 Tides are the rising and falling of waters in the oceans. 潮汐是指海水的高低起伏。
05	**water level** [`wɔtɚ `lɛvḷ]	(n.) 水平面　*high/low water level 高／低水位 At low tide, the water level drops. 退潮時，水平面會下降。
06	**ocean current** [`oʃən `kɜənt]	(n.) 大洋環流　*warm ocean current 暖洋流 Ocean currents are a continuous, directed movement of ocean water. 大洋環流是指海水經由引導而持續不斷的流動。
07	**trench** [trɛntʃ]	(n.) 溝渠；戰壕 (v.) 挖溝；挖戰壕　*trench warfare 塹壕戰 A trench is a deep hole in the ocean that can go down for miles. 溝渠是指一個在海裡深達好幾哩的洞。
08	**plankton** [`plæŋktən]	(n.) 浮游生物　*marine plankton 海洋浮游生物 Many creatures, like whales, feed on plankton in the oceans. 鯨魚等生物都是以海中浮游生物為生。
09	**water pollution** [`wɔtɚ pə`luʃən]	(n.) 水污染　*air/noise pollution 空氣／噪音汙染 Water pollution is making the seas and oceans dirty nowadays. 水污染把現今的海洋變髒了。
10	**coral reef** [`kɔrəl rif]	(n.) 珊瑚礁　*coral reef ecosystems 珊瑚礁生態系 Coral reefs are places that have huge amounts of sea life. 珊瑚礁是有大量海洋生物的地方。

The Undersea World

fish

coral reef

high tide

low tide

rise	上升
	When the tide rises, the water level gets higher. 漲潮時，水平面會上升。
fall	下降
	When the tide falls, the water level gets lower. 退潮時，水平面會下降。

move	推動；移動
	Ocean currents move water in a particular direction.
	大洋環流以特定的方向推動著水。
carry	輸送；運送
	Ocean currents carry water in a particular direction.
	大洋環流以特定的方向輸送著水。

catch	捕捉
	The fishermen are trying to catch some fish. 漁夫正在努力捕捉一些魚。
fish for	尋找；搜尋
	The fishermen are fishing for tuna. 漁夫正在尋找鮪魚的蹤跡。

Word Families ⊙ 055

salt water	鹹水；海水
	Seas and oceans have salt water. 海水是鹹水。
fresh water	淡水
	Rivers, lakes, and ponds have fresh water. 河水、湖水、池水是淡水。

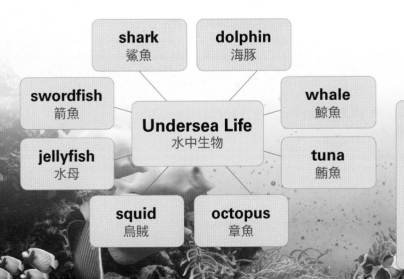

shark 鯊魚
dolphin 海豚
swordfish 箭魚
whale 鯨魚
Undersea Life 水中生物
jellyfish 水母
tuna 鮪魚
squid 烏賊
octopus 章魚

The Five Oceans 五大海洋

Pacific Ocean 大平洋
Atlantic Ocean 大西洋
Indian Ocean 印度洋
Arctic Ocean 北極海；北冰洋
Antarctic Ocean 南極海；南冰洋

Checkup

A Write l 請依提示寫出正確的英文單字。

1	海洋	_____	9	上升 _____
2	潮水	_____	10	下降 _____
3	岸	_____	11	水平面 _____
4	大洋環流	_____	12	海豚 _____
5	浮游生物	_____	13	鮪魚 _____
6	鹹水；海水	_____	14	溝渠 _____
7	淡水	_____	15	水汙染 _____
8	海底的	_____	16	珊瑚礁 _____

B Complete the Sentences l 請在空格中填入最適當的答案，並視情況做適當的變化。

ocean	tide	water pollution	undersea
salt water	plankton	coral reef	water level

1 _____ are the rising and falling of waters in the oceans.
潮汐是指海水的高低起伏。

2 Can you name the world's five _____ ? 你可以說出世界五大海洋的名字嗎？

3 Many sea creatures feed on _____ in the oceans.
許多海洋生物都是以海裡的浮游生物為生。

4 Seas and oceans have _____ _____. 海水是鹹水。

5 When the tide falls, the _____ _____ gets lower. 退潮時，水平面會下降。

6 _____ _____ is making the seas and oceans dirty.
水污染把現今的海洋變髒了。

7 Many kinds of plants and animals live in the _____ world.
海底世界住了多種植物和動物。

8 _____ _____ are places that have huge amounts of sea life.
珊瑚礁是有大量海洋生物的地方。

C Read and Choose l 閱讀下列句子，並且選出最適當的答案。

1 When the tide (rises | falls), the water level gets higher.

2 At low tide, the water level (drops | rises).

3 The (undersea | shore) is where the sea and land meet.

4 Ocean currents (carry | catch) water in a particular direction.

D Look, Read, and Write | 看圖並且依照提示，在空格中填入正確答案。

 1 ▸ water in rivers and lakes

_____

 3 ▸ where fish and sea animals live

_____

 2 ▸ a deep hole in the ocean that can go down for miles

_____

 4 ▸ where the sea and land meet

_____

E Read and Answer | 閱讀並且回答下列問題。 056

Fishing and Overfishing

The ocean has many different habitats for many plants and animals. It helps the earth stay healthy. So we have to be careful not to hurt the ocean.

Many people around the world enjoy eating seafood. Fishermen catch food in the ocean for us to eat. This includes shellfish as well as fish. Shellfish are animals like shrimp, clams, crabs, and lobsters. Because people eat so much seafood, there are many fishermen. Unfortunately, the fishermen are catching too many fish these days. So the number of fish in the oceans is decreasing. Many fishing grounds are getting smaller and smaller. Fishermen need to stop catching so many fish. They must give the fish time to increase their numbers.

Answer the questions.

1 What do oceans help the earth do?   _____

2 What do fishermen catch?   _____

3 How many fish are fishermen catching nowadays?   _____

4 What is happening to the fishing grounds?   _____

Key Words ⊙ 057

01	**bone** [bon]	*(n.)* 骨頭；骨骼　　*skin and bone(s) 極瘦 The human body has 206 **bones**. 人體內共有 206 根骨頭。
02	**skeleton** [ˈskɛlətn̩]	*(n.)* 骨骼；骨架 *(a.)* 骨骼的；骨幹的　　*skeleton key 萬能鑰匙 A **skeleton** is the structure of the bones in the body. 骨架是身體骨骼的結構。
03	**muscle** [ˈmʌsl̩]	*(n.)* 肌肉　　*not move a muscle 一動也不動 **Muscles** make you move; you use muscles to walk, run, and jump. 肌肉讓你能夠活動；透過肌肉你才能夠走路、跑步和跳躍。
04	**heart** [hɑrt]	*(n.)* 心；心臟　　*mind 頭腦；智力　　*broken heart 心碎　　*at heart 本質上 The **heart** pumps blood to the rest of the body. 心臟的抽唧能讓全身血液流通。
05	**blood** [blʌd]	*(n.)* 血液；血統　　*bloody (a.) 流血的；血淋淋的　　*fresh blood 新成員 **Blood** carries oxygen and nutrients to the body. 血液把氧氣和營養輸送到全身。
06	**digest** [daɪˈdʒɛst]	*(v.)* 消化　　*digest (n.) 摘要；文摘 The stomach **digests** food in the body. 胃能夠消化體內的食物。
07	**saliva** [səˈlaɪvə]	*(n.)* 唾液　　*frothy saliva 白沫 **Saliva** helps break down food in the body. 唾液有助於分解體內的食物。
08	**brain** [bren]	*(n.)* 腦；智力　　*turn sb.'s brain 令某人頭腦發昏　　*rack one's brain 絞盡腦汁 The **brain** controls the body's nervous system. 大腦控制了體內神經系統。
09	**nerve** [nɝv]	*(n.)* 神經；膽量　　*lose one's nerve 失去勇氣；變得慌張 　　　　　　　　　*have the nerve to do sth. 有勇氣做某事 **Nerves** send messages to all parts of the body. 神經把訊息傳送至身體的各個部位。
10	**germ** [dʒɝm]	*(n.)* 細菌；微生物　　*virus 病毒 Some **germs** can make you sick. 有些細菌會致病。

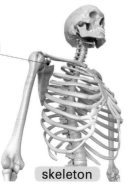

bone

skeleton

muscle

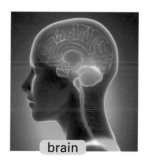

brain

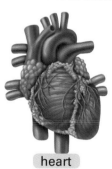

heart

| **pump** | 抽吸；灌注
A person's heart constantly **pumps** blood. 人體的心臟不斷地抽唧血液。 |
| **beat** | 打；擊
A person's heart **beats** many times a minute. 人體的心臟一分鐘跳很多下。 |

| **send** | 傳遞；發送
Nerves from the brain **send** messages throughout the body.
大腦神經把訊息傳遞到身體各部位。 |
| **carry** | 輸送；運送
Nerves from the brain **carry** messages throughout the body.
大腦神經把訊息輸送至身體各部位。 |

move	移動；搬移 Muscles let the body **move**. 肌肉讓身體能夠活動。
circulate	循環 Blood **circulates** throughout the entire body. 血液在全身體內循環。
break down	可分解；故障 The stomach **breaks** food **down** into nutrients. 胃把食物分解成營養。

Word Families 🔊 059

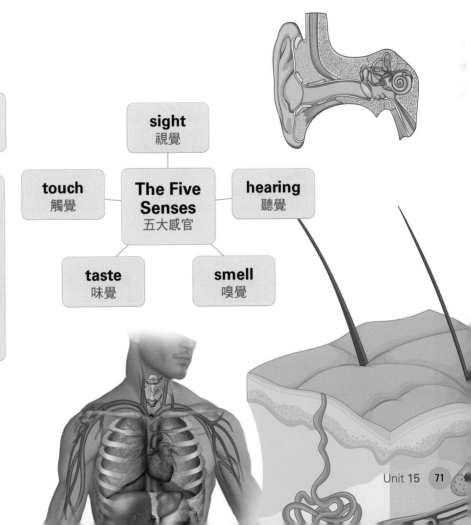

The Systems of the Body
身體系統

- **skeletal system** 骨骼系統
- **muscular system** 肌肉系統
- **circulatory system** 循環系統
- **digestive system** 消化系統
- **nervous system** 神經系統

The Five Senses
五大感官

- **sight** 視覺
- **touch** 觸覺
- **hearing** 聽覺
- **taste** 味覺
- **smell** 嗅覺

Checkup

A

Write | 請依提示寫出正確的英文單字。

1	骨頭	_____	9	消化	_____
2	骨架	_____	10	唾液	_____
3	肌肉	_____	11	抽吸；灌注	_____
4	心臟	_____	12	打；擊	_____
5	血液	_____	13	可分解；故障	_____
6	腦	_____	14	消化系統	_____
7	神經	_____	15	神經系統	_____
8	細菌	_____	16	肌肉系統	_____

B

Complete the Sentences | 請在空格中填入最適當的答案，並視情況做適當的變化。

digest	skeleton	heart	skeletal system	bone
circulate	germ	saliva	nervous system	muscle

1 The human body has 206 _____. 人體內共有 206 根骨頭。

2 A _____ is the structure of the bones. 骨架是身體骨骼的結構。

3 The brain controls the body's _____ _____. 大腦控制了體內神經系統。

4 The stomach _____ food in the body. 胃能夠消化體內的食物。

5 Some _____ can make you sick. 有些細菌會致病。

6 _____ make you move. 肌肉讓你能夠活動。

7 The _____ pumps blood to the rest of the body.
心臟的抽唧能讓全身血液流通。

8 Blood _____ throughout a person's entire body. 血液在全身體內循環。

C

Read and Choose | 閱讀下列句子，並且選出最適當的答案。

1 A person's heart constantly (pumps | beats) blood.

2 Nerves from the brain (move | send) messages throughout the body.

3 Saliva helps (break down | circulate) food in the body.

4 Blood (digests | carries) oxygen and nutrients to the body.

Look, Read, and Write | 看圖並且依照提示，在空格中填入正確答案。

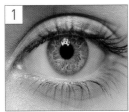 1
▸ the sense of seeing

_____

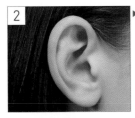 2
▸ the sense of hearing

_____

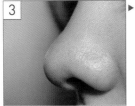 3
▸ the sense of smelling

_____

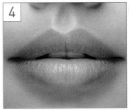 4
▸ the sense of tasting

_____

 5
▸ the sense of touching

_____

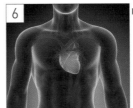 6
▸ the organ in your chest that makes blood flow around your body

_____

 E

Read and Answer | 閱讀並且回答下列問題。 🔊 060

Staying Healthy

A person's body is like a machine. It has many parts that help keep it running. If these parts are running well, a person will be healthy. But sometimes a person's body breaks down. Then that person gets sick.

Many times, germs make a person sick. When germs attack a body, it needs to fight back. Sometimes, the person's body alone can defeat the germs. Other times, the person might need medicine from a doctor to get better. Fortunately, many medicines can kill germs and help bodies become healthy again.

Fill in the blanks.

1   The body is like a _____.

2   A person's body sometimes _____ down.

3   _____ sometimes make people sick.

4   Doctors give people _____ to make them better.

A

Write | 請依提示寫出正確的英文單字。

1	植物	_____	11 生長；成長	_____
2	葉子	_____	12 下雨	_____
3	莖	_____	13 下雪	_____
4	根	_____	14 落下；秋天	_____
5	季節	_____	15 水平面	_____
6	天氣	_____	16 鯨魚	_____
7	棲息地	_____	17 味覺	_____
8	生物	_____	18 生活在；居住在	_____
9	骨架	_____	19 消化	_____
10	肌肉	_____	20 神經系統	_____

B

Choose the Correct Word | 請選出與鋪底字意思相近的答案。

1 A plant needs air, water, and sunlight to grow.

   a. get bigger   b. carry   c. absorb

2 Roots take in water from the soil.

   a. carry   b. absorb   c. make food

3 Animals need food, water, and oxygen to stay alive.

   a. change   b. adapt   c. survive

4 Animals and plants adapt to survive in their environment.

   a. go through   b. change   c. live

C

Complete the Sentences | 請在空格中填入最適當的答案，並視情況做適當的變化。

tide	season	habitat	stem

1 _____ carry water and nutrients from the roots. 莖會從根部取得水分和養分。

2 The weather changes with each _____. 每個季節的天氣都會變換。

3 _____ are the rising and falling of waters in the oceans.
潮汐是指海水的高低起伏。

4 A _____ is a place where animals and plants live.
棲息地是動物和植物居住的地方。

CHAPTER 4

Science ②

Unit 16 How Can Matter Change?

Key Words ● 061

01	**solid** [ˋsɑlɪd]	(n.) 固體 (a.) 堅固的；固體的　*(as) solid as a rock 堅若磐石 Solids are hard objects that can be touched. 固體是指堅硬、摸得到的物體。
02	**liquid** [ˋlɪkwɪd]	(n.) 液體 (a.) 液態的；透明的　*liquid diet 流質膳食 *washing liquid 洗衣精 Water is a liquid. 水是液體。
03	**gas** [gæs]	(n.) 氣體；瓦斯；〔美口〕汽油　*gas pedal【美】（汽車）油門 The air in the sky and inside balloons is a gas. 天空中與氣球裡的空氣都是氣體。
04	**matter** [ˋmætɚ]	(n.) 物質；事情　*no matter what 不管什麼 Everything in the world is made of different forms of matter. 世界上所有的事物都是由不同狀態的物質所組成的。
05	**form** [fɔrm]	(n.) 形狀；形式 (v.) 構成　*in the form of 以……的形式 Ice is water in its solid form. 冰是固態的水。
06	**state** [stet]	(n.) 狀態；情況 (v.) 陳述　*stated 指定的 There are three states of matter: solid, liquid, and gas. 物質有三種狀態：固體、液體和氣體。
07	**change** [tʃendʒ]	(v.) 改變 (n.) 改變；零錢　*a change for the better 變好 What causes water to change into a gas? 什麼會使水變為氣體？
08	**heat** [hit]	(v.) 加熱；變熱 (n.) 熱度　*heating pad 熱敷墊；電毯 You can heat a solid to turn it into a liquid. 固體加熱後就能夠變成液體。
09	**cool** [kul]	(v.) 冷卻；使冷靜下來 (a.) 涼快的；冷靜的；酷的　*cool sb. off（使某人）冷靜 You can cool a gas to change it into a liquid. 氣體冷卻後就能夠變成液體。
10	**boil** [bɔɪl]	(v.) 沸騰；烹煮　*boil away（使某物）燒乾；使（某物）蒸發 If you boil water, it changes from a liquid to a gas. 水煮沸後就會從液體變成氣體。

liquid
water

juice

solid
ice

popsicle

gas
steam
(= water vapor)

touch	觸摸；接觸 It is possible to touch solid matter. 固態物體是可以摸得到的。
feel	感覺 It is possible to feel solid matter. 固態物體是可以感覺得到的。
change into	變成…… Juice can change into a popsicle. 果汁可以變成冰棒。
become	成為…… Juice can become a popsicle. 果汁可以成為冰棒。
freeze	結冰；凝固 Very cold temperatures can freeze water. 水在非常寒冷的溫度下會結冰。
melt	融化；溶化；熔化 Very hot temperatures can melt ice. 冰在非常高溫的情況下會融化。

Word Families ⊙ 063

Solids 固體	**ice** 冰塊	**gold** 黃金	**silver** 銀	**car** 汽車	**book** 書

Liquids 液體	**water** 水	**juice** 果汁	**milk** 牛奶	**coke** 可樂	**beer** 啤酒

Gases 氣體	**air** 空氣	**steam** 蒸氣	**oxygen** 氧氣	**hydrogen** 氫氣	**helium** 氦氣

Checkup

A

Write | 請依提示寫出正確的英文單字。

1	固體	_____	9	變成……	c_____
2	液體	_____	10	沸騰	_____
3	氣體	_____	11	觸摸	_____
4	物質	_____	12	感覺	_____
5	形狀	_____	13	成為……	b_____
6	狀態	_____	14	結冰	_____
7	加熱	_____	15	融化	_____
8	冷卻	_____	16	空氣	_____

B

Complete the Sentences | 請在空格中填入最適當的答案，並視情況做適當的變化。

matter	solid	gas	state	boil
melt	change	touch	cool	liquid

1 Water is a _____. 水是液體。

2 There are three _____ of matter: solid, liquid, and gas.
   物質有三種狀態：固體、液體和氣體。

3 The air in the sky and inside balloons is a _____.
   天空中與氣球裡的空氣都是氣體。

4 If you _____ water, it changes from a liquid to a gas.
   水煮沸後就會從液體變成氣體。

5 Very hot temperatures can _____ ice. 冰在非常高溫的情況下會融化。

6 What causes water to _____ into a gas? 什麼會使水變為氣體？

7 _____ are hard objects that can be touched. 固體是指堅硬、摸得到的物體。

8 It is possible to _____ solid matter. 固態物體是可以摸得到的。

C

Read and Choose | 閱讀下列句子，並且選出最適當的答案。

1 Very cold temperatures can (melt | freeze) water.

2 Ice is water in its (liquid | solid) form.

3 You can (heat | cool) ice to turn it into water.

4 You can (cool | heat) a gas to change it into a liquid.

D Look, Read, and Write | 看圖並且依照提示，在空格中填入正確答案。

Is it a solid, a liquid, or a gas? Write the correct form of matter for each item.

 ▸ water

_____

 ▸ ice

_____

 ▸ air

_____

 ▸ lemon juice

_____

 ▸ steam

_____

 ▸ gold

_____

E Read and Answer | 閱讀並且回答下列問題。 🔊 064

How Can Water Change?

Water has three forms. It can be a solid, a liquid, or a gas. Why does it change? It changes because of the temperature. Water's normal state is liquid. But water sometimes becomes a solid. Why? It gets too cold. Water freezes when heat is taken away from it. Water in its solid form is called ice. Also, sometimes water becomes a gas. Why? It gets too hot. Water boils when its temperature gets high enough. Then it turns into steam. This steam is a gas. When water is a gas, it is called water vapor.

States of Matter

SOLID   LIQUID   GAS

Fill in the blanks.

1 Water can be a solid, a _____, or a gas.

2 Water's normal _____ is liquid.

3 Solid water is called _____.

4 Water _____ when it gets hot.

How Long? How Tall? 多長？多高？

measuring tape

Key Words 🔊 065

01	**measure** [ˈmɛʒɚ]	*(v.)* 測量；估量 *(n.)* 度量單位 *have/take/get someone's measure 量某人的尺寸 People use rulers to measure length. 人們用尺來測量長度。
02	**inch** [ɪntʃ]	*(n.)* 英吋 *inch by inch 慢慢地；一點一點地 You use inches when you measure your waist size. 測量腰圍尺寸時會以英吋為單位。
03	**foot** [fʊt]	*(n.)* 英尺；腳；足（複數形為 feet） *on foot 步行 One foot is about 30 centimeters. 一英尺約為 30 公分。
04	**pound** [paʊnd]	*(n.)*（重量單位）磅 *kilogram (kg) 公斤（1 pound = 0.45kg） People use ounces and pounds for weight in the United States. 美國人以盎司和磅來測量重量。
05	**height** [haɪt]	*(n.)* 高度；身高 *at full height 挺直 Use feet or centimeters to measure height. 以英尺或公分來測量高度。
06	**weight** [wet]	*(n.)* 重量；體重 *under weight 過輕 People measure weight with a scale. 人們用磅秤來測量重量。
07	**length** [lɛŋθ]	*(n.)* 長度 *at full length 全身伸直 People use inches and feet for length in the United States. 美國人以英吋和英尺來測量長度。
08	**distance** [ˈdɪstəns]	*(n.)* 距離；遠處 *keep one's distance from 與……保持距離 Use meters or miles when you measure distance. 以公尺或英里來測量距離。
09	**temperature** [ˈtɛmprətʃɚ]	*(n.)* 溫度；體溫 *take sb.'s temperature（以溫度計）量某人的體溫 The temperature tells you how hot or cold something is. 溫度代表了某事物有多熱或多冷。
10	**thermometer** [θɚˈmɑmətɚ]	*(n.)* 溫度計 A thermometer measures temperature. 溫度計用來測量溫度。

Measure

height

weight

length

temperature

be measured by	以……來測量 Length is measured by a ruler. 用尺來測量長度。
be calculated by [ˈkælkjəˌletɪd]	以……來計算 Weight is calculated by a scale. 用磅秤來測量重量。
take	量取；記錄 People take a temperature by using a thermometer. 人們用溫度計來測量溫度。
fill	裝滿；填滿 Fill the container with two cups of the liquid. 在容器裡裝入兩杯液體。
pour	倒；灌；注 Pour two cups of the liquid into the container. 把兩杯液體倒入容器內。

Word Families 🔊 067

---

measure 測量；計量

measure height 測量高度	measure length 測量長度
measure weight 測量重量	measure distance 測量距離
measure temperature 測量溫度	measure the amount of sugar 測量糖分

How 有多……

How much? 有多少？	How long? 有多長？	How tall? 有多高？
How high? 有多高？	How far? 有多遠？	How hot? 有多熱？
How cold? 有多冷？		

Weights and measures 重量單位和度量單位

meter 公尺（1 公尺 = 100 公分）	kilogram 公斤（1 公斤 = 1,000 公克）
liter 公升（1 公升 = 1,000 c.c.）	gallon 加侖（1 加侖 = 4.4 公升）
tablespoon 湯匙（1 湯匙 = 15 毫升）	teaspoon 茶匙（1 茶匙 = 1/3 湯匙）

A

Write | 請依提示寫出正確的英文單字。

1	測量	_____	9	磅	_____
2	英吋	_____	10	英尺	_____
3	長度	_____	11	量取	_____
4	距離	_____	12	裝滿	_____
5	高度	_____	13	倒；灌	_____
6	溫度	_____	14	測量高度	_____
7	溫度計	_____	15	測量長度	_____
8	重量	_____	16	測量分量	_____

B

Complete the Sentences | 請在空格中填入最適當的答案，並視情況做適當的變化。

weight	measure	height	inch	temperature
fill	calculate	distance	foot	thermometer

1 People use rulers to _____ length. 人們用尺來測量長度。

2 People measure _____ with a scale. 人們用磅秤來測量重量。

3 One _____ is about 30 centimeters. 一英尺約為 30 公分。

4 Use feet or centimeters to measure _____. 以英尺或公分來測量高度。

5 The _____ tells you how hot or cold something is.
溫度代表了某事物有多熱或多冷。

6 Temperature is measured by a _____. 溫度計用來測量溫度。

7 _____ the container with two cups of the liquid. 在容器裡裝入兩杯液體。

8 Weight is _____ by a scale. 用磅秤來測量重量。

C

Read and Choose | 閱讀下列句子，並且選出最適當的答案。

1 Use (meters | kilograms) when you measure distance.

2 You use (inches | feet) when you measure your waist size.

3 People use ounces and (pounds | feet) for weight in the United States.

4 People (make | take) a temperature by using a thermometer.

D

Look, Read, and Write | 看圖並且依照提示，在空格中填入正確答案完成句子。

 1 ▶ Use feet or centimeters to measure your

_____.

 2 ▶ Use inches or centimeters to measure

_____.

 3 ▶ Use a scale when you measure

_____.

 4 ▶ Use a thermometer to measure

_____.

E

Read and Answer | 閱讀並且回答下列問題。 🔊 068

Measuring Food

It's time to make some cookies. We have all of the ingredients. Now, we need to measure everything before we start cooking.

First, we need 1 cup of butter. After that, we need $\frac{3}{4}$ cup of white sugar, the same amount of brown sugar, and $2\frac{1}{4}$ cups of flour. We also need $1\frac{1}{2}$ teaspoons of vanilla extract, 1 teaspoon of baking soda, and $\frac{1}{2}$ teaspoon of salt. We have to measure $1\frac{1}{2}$ cups of chocolate chips, too. Finally, we need 2 eggs. Now we have measured all of our ingredients. Let's start cooking.

Answer the questions.

1   What is the person making?   _____

2   How much brown sugar is needed?   _____

3   How many chocolate chips are needed?   _____

4   How many eggs are needed?   _____

Key Words 🔊 069

| 01 | **electricity** [ˌɪlɛkˈtrɪsətɪ] | *(n.)* 電；電流；電力；電學　*static electricity【物】靜電 |

Electricity runs machines like TVs, computers, and refrigerators.
電能使電視、電腦和冰箱等機器運作。

| 02 | **energy** [ˈɛnədʒɪ] | *(n.)* 能量；活力；〔複〕精力　*alternative energy（太陽能等的）替代能源 |

Electricity is a form of energy. 電是能量的一種形式。

| 03 | **current** [ˈkɝənt] | *(n.)* 電流；水流；氣流；潮流；趨勢　*direct/alternating current 直／交流電 |

An electric current runs through a wire. 電流流經一條電線。

| 04 | **lightning** [ˈlaɪtnɪŋ] | *(n.)* 閃電 *(a.)* 閃電的　*lightning strike 雷擊 |

A lightning bolt is a powerful form of electricity.
閃電是一種很強大的電力形式。

| 05 | **wire** [waɪr] | *(n.)* 電線；金屬線；電纜　*wired 有（電）線的　*barbed wire 有刺鐵絲網 |

What's the job of a wire? 電線的作用是什麼？

| 06 | **battery** [ˈbætərɪ] | *(n.)* 電池　*out of battery 沒電　*dead battery 電池沒電 |

A battery can store electricity inside it. 電池能夠儲存電力。

| 07 | **switch** [swɪtʃ] | *(n.)* 開關 *(v.)* 開或關；轉換　*switch on/off 開／關（電器） |

What happens when you turn on a switch?
打開電源後會產生何種結果呢？

| 08 | **lightbulb** [ˈlaɪtbʌlb] | *(n.)* 電燈泡 |

The lightbulb lights up when you turn on the switch.
當你打開電源後，電燈泡會亮起來。

| 09 | **experiment** [ɪkˈspɛrəmənt] | *(n.) (v.)* 實驗；試驗　*carry out/conduct/do/perform an experiment 做實驗 |

Let's do an experiment. Try to turn on the bulb.
我們來做個實驗，試著將電燈泡開啟。

| 10 | **power company** [ˈpaʊɚ ˈkʌmpənɪ] | *(n.)* 電力公司 |

An electric power company makes electricity. 電力公司製造電力。

outlet
switch

socket
lightbulb

plug

Power Verbs 🔊 070

turn on　（電視等機器）開啟
Turn on the light. 打開電燈。

turn off　（電視等機器）關掉
Turn off the light. 關掉電燈。

flow　（河水等）流動
Electricity can flow through wires. 電能夠流經電線。

travel　（光、聲音等）行進；傳導
Electricity can travel through wires. 電能夠藉由電線傳導。

move　搬動；移動
Electricity can move through wires. 電能夠藉由電線轉移。

Word Families 🔊 071

outlet　電源插座
Plug the TV into a wall outlet. 把電視的電線插入牆上的插座裡。

socket　插座；插口
Plug the TV into the electrical socket. 把電視的電線插入插座裡。

plug　插頭；插塞
Electricity moves from outlets through plugs and wires.
電從插座經由插頭和電線傳導。

Electric
電的；用電的；電動的

electric current
電流

electric power
電力

electric light
電燈

electric guitar
電吉他

Electrical
與電有關的；電的；用電的

electrical appliance
電器

electrical equipment
電子設備

electrical goods
電子產品

electrical outlet
電源插座

Battery
電池；蓄電池

A battery
A 電池

AA battery
AA 電池（3 號電池）

AAA battery
AAA 電池（4 號電池）

car battery
車電瓶

lithium battery
鋰電池

cell phone battery
手機電池

Checkup

A

Write | 請依提示寫出正確的英文單字。

1	電	_____	9	電流	_____
2	能量	_____	10	電力公司	_____
3	閃電	_____	11	（電視等機器）開啟	_____
4	電線	_____	12	（電視等機器）關掉	_____
5	電池	_____	13	（河水等）流動	_____
6	開關	_____	14	搬動；移動	_____
7	電燈泡	_____	15	電力	_____
8	實驗	_____	16	手機電池	_____

B

Complete the Sentences | 請在空格中填入最適當的答案，並視情況做適當的變化。

current	lightbulb	battery	switch	experiment
electricity	wire	energy	flow	lightning bolt

1 An electric _____ runs through a wire. 電流流經一條電線。

2 A _____ can store electricity inside it. 電池能夠儲存電力。

3 What happens when you turn on a _____? 打開電源後會產生何種結果呢？

4 Electricity is a form of _____. 電是能量的一種形式。

5 _____ runs machines like TVs and computers.
電能使電視和電腦等機器運作。

6 A _____ is a powerful form of electricity. 閃電是一種很強大的電力形式。

7 Let's do an _____. Try to turn on the bulb.
我們來做個實驗。試著將電燈泡開啟。

8 The _____ lights up when you turn on the switch.
當你打開電源後，電燈泡會亮起來。

C

Read and Choose | 閱讀下列句子，並且選出最適當的答案。

1 Electricity can (flow | plug) through wires.

2 (Plug | Move) the TV into a wall outlet.

3 TVs, computers, and refrigerators are (electric power | electrical appliances).

4 An electric power company makes (electricity | electrical equipment).

Look, Read, and Write | 看圖並且依照提示，在空格中填入正確答案。

What's the name of each picture? Put the correct names in the blanks.

1  ▶ _____	4  ▶ _____
2  ▶ _____	5  ▶ _____
3  ▶ _____	6  ▶ _____

E

Read and Answer | 閱讀並且回答下列問題。 072

Benjamin Franklin

Benjamin Franklin was a great American scientist. He lived more than 200 years ago. He was very curious about lightning. He thought that it was electricity. But he wasn't sure. So he decided to do an experiment.

Franklin tied a metal key to a kite. Then he waited for a storm to begin. He flew the kite in the storm. Lightning was striking in the area. Electric charges from the lightning got on the key. When Franklin touched the key, he got shocked. He had just proved that lightning was a form of electricity!

Fill in the blanks.

1   Benjamin Franklin was a _____.

2   Franklin believed that _____ was electricity.

3   Franklin flew a _____ in a storm.

4   When Franklin touched the _____, he got shocked.

Key Words 🔊 073

01	**Mercury** [ˈmɝkjərɪ]	*(n.)* 水星 Mercury is the closest planet to the sun. 水星是距離太陽最近的行星。
02	**Venus** [ˈvinəs]	*(n.)* 金星 Venus is the second planet from the sun. 金星是距離太陽第二個位置的行星。
03	**Earth** [ɝθ]	*(n.)* 地球；地上　　*on earth 世界上 The earth goes around the sun. 地球繞著太陽運轉。
04	**Mars** [mɑrz]	*(n.)* 火星 Some people call Mars the "red planet." 有些人稱火星為「紅色行星」。
05	**Jupiter** [ˈdʒupətɚ]	*(n.)* 木星 Jupiter is the largest planet in our solar system. 木星是太陽系中體積最大的行星。
06	**Saturn** [ˈsætɚn]	*(n.)* 土星 Saturn is surrounded by beautiful rings. 土星周遭圍繞著美麗的光環。
07	**Uranus** [ˈjuərənəs]	*(n.)* 天王星 Uranus is the seventh planet from the sun. 天王星是距離太陽第七個位置的行星。
08	**Neptune** [ˈnɛptjun]	*(n.)* 海王星 Neptune is named after the god of the sea. 海王星是以海神的名字來命名。
09	**Pluto** [ˈpluto]	*(n.)* 冥王星 Pluto has the most unique orbit. 冥王星擁有最獨一無二的運行軌道。
10	**sun** [sʌn]	*(n.)* 太陽　　*get/catch some sun 曬太陽 The sun has 8 planets going around it. 共有八顆行星圍繞著太陽。

The Solar System

rise　　　上升；（河、川）發源；（事件）發生
　　　　　　The sun is **rising** over the mountain. 太陽升起，高掛天空。

come up　　太陽升起；發生
　　　　　　The sun is **coming up** over the mountain. 太陽升起，高掛天空。

set　　　　使處於；使坐落；落下
　　　　　　The sun **sets** in the west. 日落西方。

go down　　下降；落下
　　　　　　The sun **goes down** in the west. 太陽西下。

orbit　　　（天體等的）運行軌道
[ˋɔrbɪt]　　　The earth **orbits** the sun. 地球繞著太陽運行。

go around　繞……轉
　　　　　　The earth **goes around** the sun. 地球繞著太陽。

star　　　星；恆星；（日、月等）天體
　　　　　　Did you know that the sun is a **star**? 你知道太陽是一顆恆星嗎？

comet　　　彗星
　　　　　　Halley's **Comet** is going to come back in 2061. 哈雷彗星將於 2061 年重返。

moon　　　月球；月亮
　　　　　　The first man on the **moon** was Neil Armstrong.
　　　　　　第一位登上月球的人是尼爾·阿姆斯壯。

planet　　　行星
　　　　　　There are 8 **planets** in our solar system. 太陽系中共有八顆行星。

satellite　　衛星；人造衛星
[ˋsætḷ͵aɪt]　　*Explorer 1* was the first **satellite** of the United States.
　　　　　　探險家一號是美國第一顆人造衛星。

space station 太空站 — Space 太空 — space shuttle 太空梭
space tour 太空旅遊 — space travel 太空旅行

Checkup

A

Write | 請依提示寫出正確的英文單字。

1	水星	_____	9	繞……轉	_____
2	金星	_____	10	（天體等的）運行軌道	_____
3	地球	_____	11	行星	_____
4	火星	_____	12	彗星	_____
5	木星	_____	13	人造衛星	_____
6	土星	_____	14	太空梭	_____
7	天王星	_____	15	太空站	_____
8	海王星	_____	16	下降；落下	_____

B

Complete the Sentences | 請在空格中填入最適當的答案，並視情況做適當的變化。

star	go down	Mercury	Pluto	Venus
Saturn	Uranus	Neptune	Mars	moon

1 The sun _____ _____ in the west. 太陽西下。

2 Did you know that the sun is a _____? 你知道太陽是一顆恆星嗎？

3 _____ is the second planet from the sun. 金星是距離太陽第二個位置的行星。

4 _____ has the most unique orbit. 冥王星擁有最獨一無二的運行軌道。

5 _____ is surrounded by beautiful rings. 土星周圍圍繞著美麗的光環。

6 _____ is the seventh planet from the sun. 天王星是距離太陽第七個位置的行星。

7 _____ is named after the god of the sea. 海王星是以海神的名字來命名。

8 The first man on the _____ was Neil Armstrong.
第一位登上月球的人是尼爾·阿姆斯壯。

C

Read and Choose | 閱讀下列句子，並且選出最適當的答案。

1 The earth (goes around | goes down) the sun.

2 The sun (rises | sets) in the west.

3 There are 8 (planets | comets) in our solar system.

4 *Explorer 1* was the first (planet | satellite) of the United States.

D

Look, Read, and Write | 看圖並且依照提示，在空格中填入正確答案。

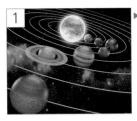

1 ▶ to go around
_____

4 ▶ the "red planet"
_____

2 ▶ to come up
_____

5 ▶ surrounded by beautiful rings
_____

3 ▶ to go down
_____

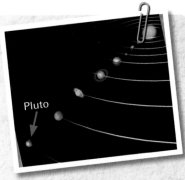

6 ▶ the largest planet in the solar system
_____

E

Read and Answer | 閱讀並且回答下列問題。 🔊 076

Is Pluto a planet?

The solar system is the sun and the planets going around the sun. There are eight planets in it. In order of distance from the sun, they are: Mercury, Venus, Earth, Mars, Jupiter, Saturn, Uranus, and Neptune. Scientists used to consider Pluto the ninth planet in the solar system. But they do not think that way now. Instead, they consider Pluto to be a minor planet. There are many objects like Pluto in the outer solar system. And scientists don't think they are planets. So they don't consider Pluto a planet anymore.

Pluto

What is true? Write T (true) or F (false).

1   There are nine planets in the solar system.   _____
2   Saturn is the fifth planet from the sun.   _____
3   Pluto is considered the ninth planet in the solar system.   _____
4   There are many objects similar to Pluto in the outer solar system.   _____

Key Words 🔊 077

01 surface
[ˈsɝfɪs]

(n.) 表面 (a.) 表面的　*surface mail 普通平信郵件

The earth's **surface** is covered with land and water.
地球表面覆蓋著土壤和水。

02 layer
[ˈleɚ]

(n.) 地層；層 (v.) 堆積成層　*ozone layer【氣】臭氧層

The earth has many different **layers**. 地球有許多不同的地層。

03 crust
[krʌst]

(n.) 地殼；麵包皮；硬外皮；外殼　*earn one's crust 掙錢糊口
*upper crust【口】上流社會

The earth's **crust** is its outer layer. 地殼是地球的最外層。

04 mantle
[ˈmæntl̩]

(n.) 地幔（位於地殼之下，地核之上）

The **mantle** is the largest part of the earth. 地幔佔地球的比例最大。

05 core
[kor]

(n.) 核心；果核；精髓；中心部分　*be rotten to the core 壞透了

The center of the earth is the **core**. 地球的中心稱為核心。

06 volcano
[vɑlˈkeno]

(n.) 火山　*active volcano 活火山

When a **volcano** erupts, it spews a lot of ash and lava.
火山爆發時，會噴出許多灰末和熔岩。

07 lava
[ˈlɑvə]

(n.) 熔岩；火山岩

Lava is the hot, melted rock that a volcano spews.
火山噴出的高溫、熔化的岩石稱為火山岩。

08 hot spring
[hɑt sprɪŋ]

(n.) 溫泉

There are many **hot springs** near volcanoes. 火山附近有許多溫泉口。

09 mineral
[ˈmɪnərəl]

(n.) 礦物 (a.) 礦物的　*mineral water 礦泉水　*mineral oil 礦物油

All rocks have many different kinds of **minerals**.
所有的岩石都含有多種不同的礦物。

10 pole
[pol]

(n.) 極地；柱；竿

There are two **poles** on Earth: the North **Pole** and the South **Pole**.
地球有兩極：北極和南極。

Inside the earth

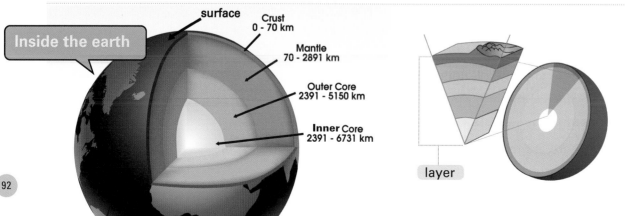

surface
Crust
0 - 70 km
Mantle
70 - 2891 km
Outer Core
2391 - 5150 km
Inner Core
2391 - 6731 km
layer

⊙ 078

erupt
（火山）噴出；爆發
The volcano is getting ready to erupt. 火山準備要爆發了。

spew [spju]
噴出；放出
The volcano spewed gas and ash. 火山噴出了沼氣和灰末。

melt
融化；熔化
Lava can melt almost anything it touches.
岩漿能夠把任何所觸及的事物都熔化。

be covered with
覆蓋著……
The volcano area is covered with a lot of ash and lava.
火山區覆蓋著許多灰燼和熔岩。

Word Families ⊙ 079

continent
大陸；陸地
Earth has seven continents on it. 地球上共有七塊大陸。

ocean
海洋
Of the five oceans, the Pacific Ocean is the biggest.
五大海洋中，太平洋是其中面積最廣大的。

Kinds of Rocks
岩石的種類

granite 花崗岩

marble 大理石

limestone 石灰岩

sandstone 沙岩

slate 板岩

quartz 石英

Checkup

A

Write | 請依提示寫出正確的英文單字。

1	表面	_____	9	礦物	_____
2	地層	_____	10	大陸；陸地	_____
3	核心	_____	11	海洋	_____
4	地殼	_____	12	極地	_____
5	地幔	_____	13	爆發	_____
6	火山	_____	14	噴出	_____
7	熔岩	_____	15	融化；熔化	_____
8	溫泉	_____	16	覆蓋著……	_____

B

Complete the Sentences | 請在空格中填入最適當的答案，並視情況做適當的變化。

layer	continent	volcano	erupt	spew
melt	hot spring	pole	cover	surface

1   The earth's _____ is covered with land and water. 地球表面覆蓋著土壤和水。

2   The earth has many different _____. 地球有許多不同的地層。

3   When a _____ erupts, it spews a lot of ash and lava.
火山爆發時，會噴出許多灰末和熔岩。

4   Lava can _____ almost anything it touches. 岩漿能夠把任何所觸及的事物都熔化。

5   The volcano _____ gas and ash. 火山噴出了沼氣和灰末。

6   There are many _____ _____ near volcanoes. 火山附近有許多溫泉口。

7   The volcano is getting ready to _____. 火山準備要爆發了。

8   There are two _____ on Earth: the North Pole and the South Pole.
地球有兩極：北極和南極。

C

Read and Choose | 閱讀下列句子，並且選出最適當的答案。

1   (Hot spring｜Lava) is the hot, melted rock that a volcano spews.

2   Earth has seven (oceans｜continents) on it.

3   Of the five oceans, the (Atlantic｜Pacific) Ocean is the biggest.

4   All rocks have many different kinds of (minerals｜lava).

D

Look, Read, and Write | 看圖並且依照提示，在空格中填入正確答案。

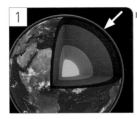
▶ the outside of
something

_____

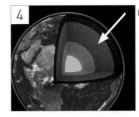
▶ The earth has three
main _____.

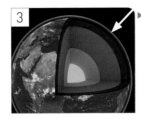
▶ the outer layer of
the earth

_____

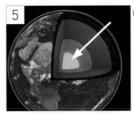
▶ the largest hot part
of the earth

_____

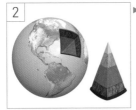
▶ the center of the
earth

_____

▶ the hot, melted rock
that a volcano spews

_____

E

Read and Answer | 閱讀並且回答下列問題。 080

The Layers of the earth

The earth is a huge planet. But it is divided into three
parts. They are the crust, mantle, and core. Each
section is different from the others.

The crust is the outermost part of the earth. That's the
surface of the earth. Everything on top of the earth — the oceans, seas, rivers,
mountains, deserts, and forests — is part of the crust. Beneath the crust, there
is a thick layer of hot, melted rock. It's called the mantle. The mantle is the
biggest section. The mantle is extremely hot. The innermost part of the earth
is the core. Part of it is solid, and part is liquid.

Answer the questions.

1   How many parts is Earth divided into?   _____
2   What is the top part of Earth called?   _____
3   What is the biggest section of Earth?   _____
4   What is the innermost part of Earth?   _____

Review Test 4

A

Write | 請依提示寫出正確的英文單字。

1	固體	_____	11	變成	c _____
2	液體	_____	12	測量高度	_____
3	氣體	_____	13	測量長度	_____
4	測量	_____	14	（電視等機器）開啟	_____
5	長度	_____	15	（河水等）流動	_____
6	電	_____	16	繞……轉	_____
7	能量	_____	17	行星	_____
8	水星	_____	18	地殼	_____
9	金星	_____	19	地幔	_____
10	表面	_____	20	核心	_____

B

Choose the Correct Word | 請選出與鋪底字意思相近的答案。

1 An electric current **moves** through a wire.

   a. flows   b. turns on   c. does

2 TVs, computers, and refrigerators are **electrical appliances**.

   a. electric power   b. electrical goods   c. electrical outlet

3 The earth **goes around** the sun.

   a. goes down   b. orbits   c. comes up

4 The sun **sets** in the west.

   a. rises   b. turns   c. goes down

C

Complete the Sentences | 請在空格中填入最適當的答案，並視情況做適當的變化。

state	Saturn	weight	layer

1 There are three _____ of matter: solid, liquid, and gas.
物質有三種狀態：固體、液體和氣體。

2 People measure _____ with a scale. 人們用磅秤來測量重量。

3 _____ is surrounded by beautiful rings. 土星周圍圍繞著美麗的光環。

4 The earth has many different _____. 地球有許多不同的地層。

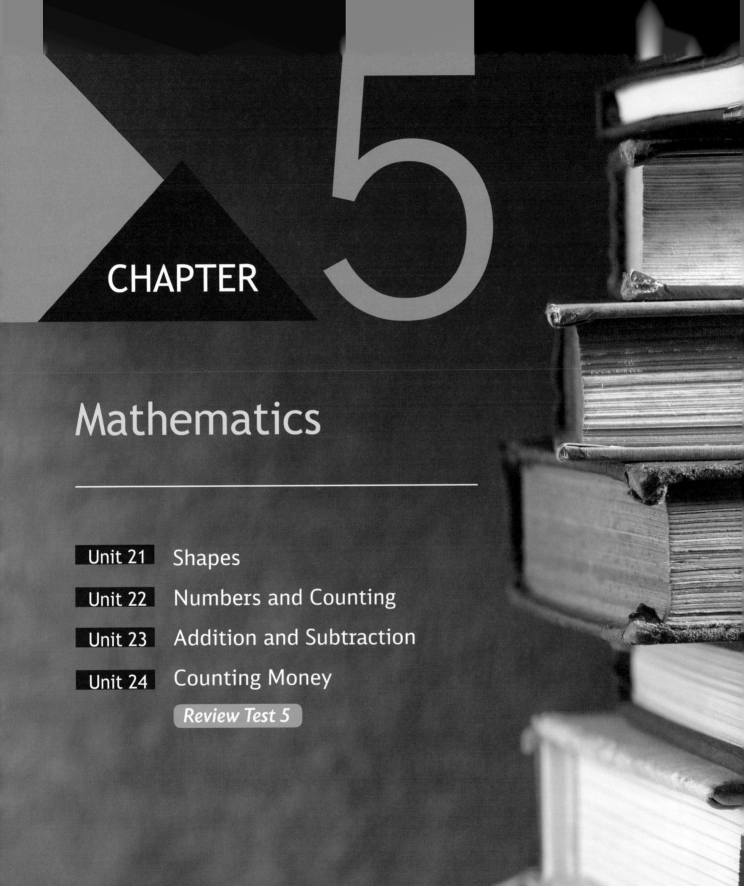

CHAPTER 5

Mathematics

Key Words 🔊 081

01	**rectangle** [rɛk`tæŋg!]	*(n.)* 長方形 A rectangle has four sides. 長方形有四個邊。
02	**square** [skwɛr]	*(n.)* 正方形；廣場 *(a.)* 正方形的　*diamond 菱形 A square has four sides of equal length. 正方形四邊等長。
03	**triangle** [`traɪ͵æŋg!]	*(n.)* 三角形；三角板；三角鐵　*right triangle 直角三角形 A shape with three sides is called a triangle. 具有三個邊的形狀稱為三角形。
04	**circle** [`sɝk!]	*(n.)* 圓形；圓圈 *(v.)* 圈出　*vicious circle 惡性循環 A circle is round and has no sides. 圓形是圓的、無邊的。
05	**oval** [`ov!]	*(a.)* 卵形的；橢圓形的 *(n.)* 卵形（物） *the Oval Office（美國白宮的）橢圓形辦公室 An egg has an oval shape. 雞蛋是橢圓形的。
06	**side** [saɪd]	*(n.)* 邊；面；側 *(a.)* 旁邊的　*side by side 肩並肩地 A square has four sides, but a triangle only has three. 正方形有四個邊，但三角形只有三邊。
07	**edge** [ɛdʒ]	*(n.)* 邊緣；刀口　*be on edge 緊張不安的 A triangle has three edges. 三角形有三條邊線。
08	**cube** [kjub]	*(n.)* 立方；立方體　*ice cube 冰塊　*sugar cube 方糖 A cube has six sides that are all the same length. 立方體共有六個等長的邊。
09	**flat shape** [flæt ʃep]	*(n.)* 平面形狀 Rectangles, triangles, and circles are flat shapes. 長方形、三角形和圓形都是平面的形狀。
10	**solid shape** [`sɑlɪd ʃep]	*(n.)* 立體形狀 Spheres and cubes are solid shapes. 球體和立方體都是立體的形狀。

Flat Shapes　circle　oval　triangle　rectangle　square

Solid Shapes　sphere　cube　cone　cylinder　pyramid

resemble
[rɪˋzæmbḷ]

像;類似
A rectangle resembles a square. 長方形類似正方形。

be similar to

相像的;類似的
A rectangle is similar to a square. 長方形和正方形很像。

differ from

不同於……
A triangle differs from a circle. 三角形不同於圓形。

be different from

和……不同
A triangle is different from a circle. 三角形和圓形不同。

sort

把……分類;區分
Let's sort the shapes into different categories.
讓我們把所有的形狀依照不同的種類分類吧。

classify

將……分類
Let's classify the shapes into different categories.
讓我們將所有的形狀依照不同的種類分類吧。

sphere
[sfɪr]

球;球體
The ball is a sphere. 球是一個圓的球體。

globe
[glob]

球;球狀物;地球儀
The earth is shaped like a globe. 地球的形狀像球狀。

pentagon
[ˋpɛntəgɑn]

五邊形
An object with five sides is a pentagon. 具有五個邊的物體稱為五邊形。

hexagon
[ˋhɛksəˏgən]

六邊形
A hexagon has six sides. 六邊形有六個邊。

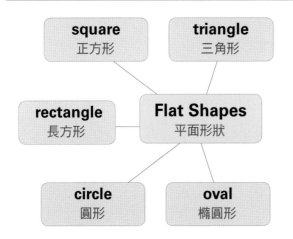

square 正方形 / triangle 三角形 / rectangle 長方形 / Flat Shapes 平面形狀 / circle 圓形 / oval 橢圓形

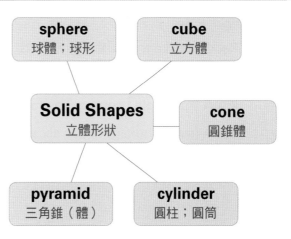

sphere 球體;球形 / cube 立方體 / Solid Shapes 立體形狀 / cone 圓錐體 / pyramid 三角錐(體) / cylinder 圓柱;圓筒

Checkup

A

Write | 請依提示寫出正確的英文單字。

1 長方形	_____	9 邊;面	_____
2 正方形	_____	10 邊緣	_____
3 三角形	_____	11 平面形狀	_____
4 圓形	_____	12 立體形狀	_____
5 橢圓形的	_____	13 圓柱;圓筒	_____
6 立方體	_____	14 球體;球形	_____
7 五邊形	_____	15 把……分類	_____
8 六邊形	_____	16 像;類似	_____

B

Complete the Sentences | 請在空格中填入最適當的答案,並視情況做適當的變化。

differ	pyramid	solid shape	edge	side
circle	globe	similar to	classify	cylinder

1 A rectangle has four _____. 長方形有四個邊。

2 A triangle has three _____. 三角形有三條邊線。

3 Spheres and cubes are _____ _____. 球體和立方體都是立體的形狀。

4 A triangle _____ from a circle. 三角形和圓形不同。

5 A _____ is round and has no sides. 圓形是圓的、無邊的。

6 A rectangle is _____ _____ a square. 長方形和正方形很像。

7 The earth is shaped like a _____. 地球的形狀像球狀。

8 Let's _____ the shapes into different categories.
讓我們將所有的形狀依照不同的種類分類吧。

C

Read and Choose | 閱讀下列句子,並且選出最適當的答案。

1 An egg has an (circle | oval) shape.

2 A (rectangle | square) has four sides of equal length.

3 A (cube | hexagon) has six sides that are all the same length.

4 Rectangles, triangles, and circles are (solid shapes | flat shapes).

Look, Read, and Write | 看圖並且依照提示，在空格中填入正確答案。

1 ▸ a shape with three sides

_____

2 ▸ shapes like circles or rectangles

_____

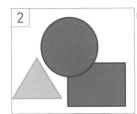
3 ▸ shapes like spheres or cubes

_____

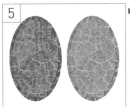
4 ▸ the shape of a ball

_____

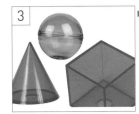
5 ▸ to be similar to

_____

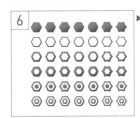
6 ▸ sort

_____

E

Read and Answer | 閱讀並且回答下列問題。 🔊 084

Five Simple Shapes

There are five basic shapes: the square, rectangle, triangle, circle, and oval. There are many other shapes, but they all resemble these five basic ones.

Every object has a certain shape. For example, a box may look like a square or rectangle. So does a cube. A piece of pizza might resemble a triangle. A soccer ball and a baseball are both circles. And eggs are oval-shaped. There are also other more complicated shapes. A mountain might resemble a pyramid. And a funnel looks like a cone.

What is true? Write T (true) or F (false).

1   A cube is one of the five basic shapes.   _____

2   Some boxes look like circles.   _____

3   An egg is shaped like an oval.   _____

4   Some mountains resemble pyramids.   _____

Numbers and Counting 數字和計數

Key Words
🔊 085

01	**zero** [ˈzɪro]	*(n.)* 零；沒有 *(a.)* 零的；沒有的　*zero in on sth. 把注意力集中在某事 Zero means nothing. 零表示什麼都沒有。
02	**dozen** [ˈdʌzn̩]	*(n.)* 一打　*score 二十；二十個 A dozen is twelve. 一打是 12 個。
03	**count** [kaʊnt]	*(v.)* 計算 *(n.)* 計算；總計　*count up 算出……的總數 Count out loud from 1 to 10. 大聲地從 1 數到 10。
04	**count by tens**	*(v.)* 數十的倍數 Let's count by tens: 10, 20, 30, 40. 我們來數十的倍數：10、20、30、40。
05	**count forward** [ˈfɔwəd]	*(v.)* 按照順序數 He can count forward from 0 to 10. 他能夠從 0 按順序數到 10。
06	**count backward** [ˈbækwəd]	*(v.)* 倒著數 She can count backward from 10 to 0. 她能夠從 10 倒著數到 0。
07	**order** [ˈɔrdɚ]	*(n.)* 順序；秩序 *(v.)* 命令；訂購；點菜　*in order 按順序；情況良好 The correct order for the first five numbers is 1-2-3-4-5. 前五個數字的正確順序為 1-2-3-4-5。
08	**compare** [kəmˈpɛr]	*(v.)* 比較　*compare with 與……相比 Compare the numbers. Then write them in the correct order. 比較數字，然後按照順序寫出來。
09	**place value** [ples ˈvælju]	*(n.)* 位值；地點值 29 means 2 tens and 9 ones; we call this place value. 29 表示 2 個十和 9 個一；我們稱之為位值。
10	**digit** [ˈdɪdʒɪt]	*(n.)* 數字　*binary digit 【電腦】二進制位，二進制數字 23 is a number with two digits: 2 tens and 3 ones. 23 是一個兩位數的數字：2 個十和 3 個一。

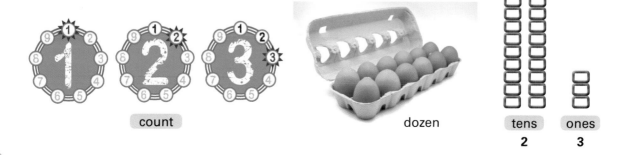

count　　　　　dozen　　　　tens　ones
　　　　　　　　　　　　　　　2　　3

Power Verbs

🔊 086

is greater than 比……大
10 is greater than 9. 10 比 9 大。

is less than 比……小
4 is less than 5. 4 比 5 小。

is equal to 和……相等；等於
6 is equal to 6. 6 等於 6。

come after 在……之後
99 comes after 98. 99 在 98 後面。

come before 在……之前
98 comes before 99. 98 在 99 前面。

Word Families

🔊 087

greater than 比……大	>	10 is greater than 5.	(10 > 5)	10 比 5 大。
less than 比……小	<	6 is less than 8.	(6 < 8)	6 比 8 小。
equal to 和……相等；等於	=	3 is equal to 3.	(3 = 3)	3 等於 3。

Ordinal Numbers
序數

first 第一
second 第二
third 第三
fourth 第四
fifth 第五
sixth 第六
seventh 第七
eighth 第八
ninth 第九
tenth 第十

Counting by Tens
數十的倍數

ten 10
twenty 20
thirty 30
forty 40
fifty 50
sixty 60
seventy 70
eighty 80
ninety 90
one hundred 100

Checkup

A

Write | 請依提示寫出正確的英文單字。

1	零	_____	
2	計算	_____	
3	比較	_____	
4	比……大	_____	
5	比……小	_____	
6	和……相等	_____	
7	第一	_____	
8	第二	_____	
9	順序	_____	
10	一打	_____	
11	數十的倍數	_____	
12	按照順序數	_____	
13	倒著數	_____	
14	位值	_____	
15	數字	_____	
16	序數	_____	

B

Complete the Sentences | 請在空格中填入最適當的答案，並視情況做適當的變化。

compare	dozen	count	less than	equal to
place value	ten	digit	order	greater

1 _____ out loud from 1 to 10. 大聲地從 1 數到 10。

2 Let's count by _____: 10, 20, 30, 40. 我們來數十的倍數：10、20、30、40。

3 _____ the two numbers. 比較這兩個數字。

4 10 is _____ than 9.　10 比 9 大。

5 6 is _____ _____ 8.　6 比 8 小。

6 50 is _____ ____ 50.　50 等於 50。

7 23 is a number with two _____: 2 tens and 3 ones.
   23 是一個兩位數的數字：2 個十和 3 個一。

8 29 means 2 tens and 9 ones; we call this _____ _____.
   29 表示 2 個十和 9 個一；我們稱之為位值。

C

Read and Choose | 閱讀下列句子，並且選出最適當的答案。

1 99 comes (after | before) 98.

2 You can count (backward | forward) from 10 to 0.

3 19 means 1 ten and (8 | 9) ones.

4 10 is (equal to | greater than) 10.

Look, Read, and Write | 看圖並且依照提示，在空格中填入正確答案。

1  ▸ to be more than

_____

2 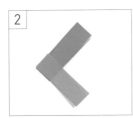 ▸ to come before in counting

_____

3  ▸ to be the same as

_____

4  ▸ to mean nothing

_____

5  ▸ twelve

_____

6 ▸ 65 is a number with two _____.

E

Read and Answer | 閱讀並且回答下列問題。 ⦿ 088

Greater and Less Than

All numbers have a certain value. So some numbers are greater than others. And some numbers are less than others.

A number that comes after another number is greater than it. For example, 6 comes after 5. So we can say, "6 is greater than 5." In math terms, we write it like this: 6 > 5. A number that comes before another number is less than it. For example, 2 comes before 3. So we can say, "2 is less than 3." In math terms, we write it like this: 2 < 3.

Fill in the blanks.

1 Some numbers are greater _____ others.

2 6 comes _____ 5.

3 5 is _____ than 4.

4 2 is _____ than 3.

Addition and Subtraction 加法和減法

01	**addition** [əˋdɪʃən]	*(n.)* 加法;附加;添加物　*in addition to 除……尚有 Addition is written using the plus sign "+" between numbers. 加法就是在數字之間寫上「＋」的符號。
02	**subtraction** [səbˋtrækʃən]	*(n.)* 減法;減去 Subtraction is written using the minus sign "-" between numbers. 減法就是在數字之間寫上「－」的符號。
03	**plus** [plʌs]	*(prep.)* 加上 *(a.)* 加的 *(n.)* 好處　*plus point 好的一面;長處 Two plus two is four. (2+2=4) 2 加 2 等於 4。
04	**minus** [ˋmaɪnəs]	*(prep.)* 減去 *(a.)* 負的 *(n.)* 負數;負號　*on the minus side 在其劣勢方面 Seven minus six is one. (7−6=1) 7 減 6 等於 1。
05	**equal** [ˋikwəl]	*(v.)* 等於 *(a.)* 相等的;平等的　*be equal to 能勝任……;等於…… Ten minus four equals six. (10−4=6) 10 減 4 等於 6。
06	**sum** [sʌm]	*(n.)* 總數 *(v.)* 計算總和;總結　*sum up 計算 The sum of three plus six is nine. (3+6=9) 3 加 6 的總和為 9。
07	**difference** [ˋdɪfərəns]	*(n.)* 差額;差距;差別　*make a difference 有影響;有關係 Find the difference of 13−2. 找出 13−2 的差值。
08	**solve** [sɑlv]	*(v.)* 解決;解答;溶解　*problem-solving 解決問題 Solve the problem by doing addition. 用加法來解這個問題。
09	**find** [faɪnd]	*(v.)* 找到;發現　*find fault with 挑剔…… Find the sum of 6+3. 找出 6 加 3 的總和。
10	**problem** [ˋprɑbləm]	*(n.)* 難題;問題　*have a problem with 在……(方面)有問題 Explain how you solved the problem. 解釋你是如何解出這個問題。

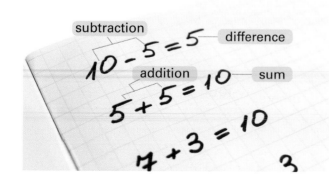

subtraction　difference
addition　sum

$10 - 5 = 5$
$5 + 5 = 10$
$7 + 3 = 10$
3

problem　solve

add	加上
	Can you add five and six together? 你可以將 5 和 6 相加嗎？
subtract	減去
	Subtract two from seven. 從 7 中減去 2。
take away	帶走；拿走
	Take away two from seven. 從 7 中拿掉 2。
equals	等於
	Ten minus four equals six. (10–4=6)　10 減 4 等於 6。
is (=)	是
	Ten minus four is six. (10–4=6)　10 減 4 是 6。
is equal to	和……相等
	Ten minus four is equal to six. (10–4=6)　10 減 4 等於 6。

a plus sign	**+**	加號
		Use a plus sign to add two numbers together. 用加號把兩個數字相加。
a minus sign	**–**	減號
		Use a minus sign to subtract one number from another. 用減號把一個數字減去另一個數字。
an equal sign	**=**	等號
		Use an equal sign to solve an addition or subtraction problem. 用等號來表示每個加法或減法問題的答案。

Counting
數；計算

eleven 11	fifteen 15	nineteen 19
twelve 12	sixteen 16	twenty 20
thirteen 13	seventeen 17	
fourteen 14	eighteen 18	

Counting Higher
數較大的數字

twenty-one 21	twenty-four 24	twenty-seven 27
twenty-two 22	twenty-five 25	twenty-eight 28
twenty-three 23	twenty-six 26	twenty-nine 29

Checkup

A

Write I 請依提示寫出正確的英文單字。

1	加法	_____	9	是	_____
2	減法	_____	10	和……相等	_____
3	加上	a_____	11	等於	_____
4	減去	s_____	12	帶走;拿走	_____
5	總數	_____	13	找到	_____
6	差額;差距	_____	14	等號	_____
7	解決;解答	_____	15	減號	_____
8	難題;問題	_____	16	加號	_____

B

Complete the Sentences I 請在空格中填入最適當的答案,並視情況做適當的變化。

problem	subtract	equal	add	find
take away	addition	minus sign	equal sign	solve

1 Ten minus four _____ six. 10 減 4 等於 6。

2 _____ the sum of 10 and 9. 找出 10 加 9 的總和是多少。

3 _____ the problem by doing addition. 用加法來解這個問題。

4 Can you _____ five and six together? 你可以將 5 和 6 相加嗎?

5 _____ _____ two from seven. 從 7 中拿掉 2。

6 Explain how you solved the _____. 解釋你是如何解出這個問題。

7 _____ is written using the plus sign between numbers.
加法就是在數字之間寫上「+」的符號。

8 Subtraction is written using the _____ _____ between numbers.
減法就是在數字之間寫上「-」的符號。

C

Read and Choose I 閱讀下列句子,並且選出最適當的答案。

1 Ten (minus | plus) four equals six.

2 Two (minus | plus) two is four.

3 Find the (difference | sum) of 13-2.

4 The (difference | sum) of three plus seven is ten.

D Look, Read, and Write | 看圖並且依照提示，在空格中填入正確答案。

What sign belongs in the squares here?

1
$$9 \ \square \ 2 = 11$$

▶ _____

4
$$5+2 \ \square \ 6$$

▶ _____

2
$$12 \ \square \ 3 = 9$$

▶ _____

5
$$5-2 \ \square \ 6$$

▶ _____

3
$$5+3 \ \square \ 6+2$$

▶ _____

6
$$6-3 \ \square \ 3-0$$

▶ _____

E Read and Answer | 閱讀並且回答下列問題。 ⊙ 092

Addition and Subtraction

Addition is adding two or more numbers together. When you add numbers together, the answer you get is called *sum*. For example, the sum of 5+2 is 7. Subtraction is taking a number away from another. Imagine you have 5 apples. You take away 2 apples and give them to your brother. How many are left? There were 5 apples, but you took away 2, so now you have 3 apples. 5-2=3. The number you have left is called the *difference*. So, the difference of 5-2 is 3.

What is NOT true?

1   Putting two numbers together is subtraction.

2   The sum of 5 plus 2 is 7.

3   5 minus 2 is 3.

4   The difference of 5-2 is 3.

Counting Money 數錢

Key Words 🔊 093

01	**money** ['mʌnɪ]	(n.) 錢；貨幣　*make money 賺錢；致富 Money can be both paper bills and coins. 紙鈔和硬幣都是指錢。
02	**value** ['vælju]	(n.) 價值 (v.) 估價；重視　*place value on 重視…… The value of a quarter is twenty-five cents. 四分之一元與 25 分等值。
03	**amount** [ə'maʊnt]	(n.) 數量；總計　*amount to 總計為 Two hundred dollars is a large amount of money. 200 元是一大筆錢。
04	**cent** [sɛnt]	(n.)（美加等國 1 元的 1%）分　*one's two cents 個人淺見 One cent has a very low value. 一分錢很廉價。
05	**penny** ['pɛnɪ]	(n.)〔英〕一便士硬幣；〔美〕一分硬幣；一小筆錢 *A penny saved is a penny earned. 積少成多。 Five pennies equal five cents. 五便士硬幣和五分硬幣相等。
06	**nickel** ['nɪkl̩]	(n.)〔美〕五分鎳幣；〔化〕鎳 (v.) 鍍鎳於　*nickel-and-dime【美】【口】便宜的 A nickel has a larger value than a penny. 五分鎳幣比一分硬幣更有價值。
07	**dime** [daɪm]	(n.) 美國或加拿大的一角硬幣　*dime store 廉價商店 A dime is worth ten cents. 一角值十分。
08	**quarter** ['kwɔrtɚ]	(n.) 25 分硬幣；四分之一；一刻鐘　*three-quarter 四分之三的 Two dimes plus a nickel equal the value of a quarter. 兩角加五分等於 25 分。
09	**half-dollar** [hæf 'dɑlɚ]	(n.) 五角硬幣 A half-dollar is worth fifty cents. 五角硬幣等於 50 分。
10	**dollar** ['dɑlɚ]	(n.)（美加等國）元　*Eurodollar 歐元 One dollar is worth one hundred cents. 一元值 100 分。

American Coins

| penny | nickel | dime | quarter | half-dollar |

exchange	兌換;交換
	Exchange five dimes for two quarters. 把五個 10 分錢兌換成兩個 25 分錢。
trade	交易;交換
	Trade five dimes for two quarters. 把五個 10 分錢換成兩個 25 分錢。

be worth	有……價值
	One dollar is worth one hundred cents. 一元值 100 分。

combine	使結合
	Combine the coins and add up their value.
	把所有硬幣結合起來,然後相加所有的價值。
combination	結合;聯合
	There are many combinations of coins. For example, one nickel plus five pennies equal the value of a dime. 硬幣有許多組合。例如,五分鎳幣加上五分錢等於一角。

Word Families ● 095

Coins 硬幣

one-cent piece　1 分錢幣	five-cent piece　5 分錢幣
ten-cent piece　10 分錢幣	twenty-five-cent piece　25 分錢幣
fifty-cent piece　50 分錢幣	

Bills 鈔票

one-dollar bill　1 元鈔票	two-dollar bill　2 元鈔票
five-dollar bill　5 元鈔票	ten-dollar bill　10 元鈔票
twenty-dollar bill　20 元鈔票	fifty-dollar bill　50 元鈔票
one-hundred-dollar bill　100 元鈔票	

American Bills

$2　$10　$50

$1　$5　$20　$100

Checkup

A Write | 請依提示寫出正確的英文單字。

1	錢；貨幣	_____
2	硬幣	_____
3	鈔票	_____
4	一分錢	_____
5	五分鎳幣	_____
6	一角硬幣	_____
7	25分硬幣	_____
8	五角硬幣	_____
9	一分硬幣	_____
10	（美加等國）元	_____
11	數量；總計	_____
12	一元鈔票	_____
13	十元鈔票	_____
14	兌換；交換	_____
15	使結合	_____
16	有……價值	_____

B Complete the Sentences | 請在空格中填入最適當的答案，並視情況做適當的變化。

amount	quarter	money	exchange	value
penny	cent	bill	be worth	combine

1 _____ can be both paper bills and coins. 紙鈔和硬幣都是指錢。

2 Two hundred dollars is a large _____ of money. 200 元是一大筆錢。

3 Two dimes plus a nickel equal a _____. 兩角加五分等於 25 分。

4 _____ ten nickels for a half-dollar. 把十個五分鎳幣兌換成一個五角硬幣。

5 The _____ of a dime is ten cents. 一角與十分等值。

6 One dollar ____ _____ one hundred cents. 一元值 100 分。

7 Six _____ equals six cents. 六便士硬幣和六分硬幣相等。

8 _____ the coins and add up their value.
把所有硬幣結合起來，然後相加所有的價值。

C Read and Answer | 閱讀並且回答下列問題。

1 What coin is worth the same as two nickels?
何種硬幣的價值等於兩個五分鎳幣？ _____

2 What coin is worth the same as 5 dimes?
何種硬幣的價值等於五角？ _____

3 What coin is worth the same as 5 cents?
何種硬幣的價值等於五分？ _____

4 What coin is worth the same as 2 dimes plus 5 cents?
何種硬幣的價值等於兩角加五分？ _____

Look, Read, and Write | 看圖並且依照提示，在空格中填入正確答案。

1  ▸ a coin worth

five cents

_____

4  ▸ a coin worth

fifty cents

_____

2  ▸ a coin worth

ten cents

_____

5  ▸ a coin worth

1/100 of a dollar

_____

3  ▸ a coin worth

twenty-five cents

_____

6  ▸ a bill worth

100 cents

_____

E

Read and Answer | 閱讀並且回答下列問題。 ◉ 096

Making Change

People use money to buy many different goods and
services. Money can be both paper bills and coins.
All bills and coins have different values. Learn to
recognize the coins so that you can know how much

they are worth. You might buy some candy at a store. It costs seventy-five
cents, so you give the clerk a dollar. One dollar is worth 100 cents. How much
change will you get back? Twenty-five cents. You'll receive one quarter. But
maybe you don't want a quarter. Tell the clerk, "I'd like two dimes and a nickel,
please." That is how you make change.

Answer the questions.

1 What do people buy with money? _____

2 What does each coin have? _____

3 How much is one quarter worth? _____

4 What coins are worth the same as a quarter? _____

Review Test 5

A

Write | 請依提示寫出正確的英文單字。

1	長方形	_____	11	加上	a_____
2	正方形	_____	12	減去	s_____
3	三角形	_____	13	硬幣	_____
4	圓形	_____	14	鈔票	_____
5	加法	_____	15	兌換	_____
6	減法	_____	16	有……價值	_____
7	總數	_____	17	比……大	_____
8	錢；貨幣	_____	18	比……小	_____
9	數量；總計	_____	19	等於	e_____
10	一打	_____	20	順序	_____

B

Choose the Correct Word | 請選出與鋪底字意思相近的答案。

1 Ten minus four **equals** six.

   a. is   b. takes away   c. subtracts

2 10 is **greater than** 9.

   a. less than   b. more than   c. equal to

3 **Subtract** two from seven.

   a. Take away   b. Add   c. Sum

C

Complete the Sentences | 請在空格中填入最適當的答案，並視情況做適當的變化。

value	edge	add	side	solve	worth

1 A rectangle has four _____. 長方形有四個邊。

2 A triangle has three _____. 三角形有三條邊線。

3 _____ the problem by doing addition. 用加法來解這個問題。

4 Can you _____ five and six together? 你可以將 5 和 6 相加嗎？

5 The _____ of a dime is ten cents. 一角值十分。

6 One dollar is _____ one hundred cents. 一元值 100 分。

CHAPTER

6

Language •
Visual Arts • Music

Key Words

🔊 097

01 spelling

[ˈspɛlɪŋ]

(n.) 拼字   *spell (n.) 咒語

A student needs good **spelling** to write words properly.
學生須有好的拼字能力才可以寫出正確的字。

02 handwriting

[ˈhændˌraɪtɪŋ]

(n.) 書寫；手寫；筆跡   *handwritten (a.) 手寫的

Nice **handwriting** is easy for people to read.
工整的手寫字體讓人們易於閱讀。

03 punctuation

[ˌpʌŋktʃʻeʃən]

(n.) 標點符號   *punctuation mark 標點符號

Punctuation marks like periods and commas are important for writing.
句號、逗號等標點符號在寫作中相當重要。

04 rule

[rul]

(n.) 規則；規定   *by rule 依照規定

There are many **rules** to speaking and writing proper English.
正統英文中，口語和寫作有許多規則。

05 grammar

[ˈɡræmɚ]

(n.) 文法   *bad grammar 錯誤的文法

Grammar is the rules of a language. 文法是一種語言的規則。

06 alphabet

[ˈælfəˌbɛt]

(n.) 字母表；字母系統   *the Roman alphabet 羅馬字母（表）

The **alphabet** goes from A to Z. 字母表是從 A 排到 Z。

07 letter

[ˈlɛtɚ]

(n.) 字母；信件   *block letters 正楷大寫字母

There are 26 **letters** in the alphabet. 字母表中共有 26 個字母。

08 sound

[saʊnd]

(n.) 聲音；音調   *sound like 聽起來像……

Each letter of the alphabet has its own unique **sound**.
字母表中的每個字母都有各自獨立的發音。

09 word

[wɝd]

(n.) 字   *wording 措辭；用語

We use **words** to express our thoughts and feelings.
我們利用文字來傳達想法和感覺。

10 sentence

[ˈsɛntəns]

(n.) 句子；判決   *life sentence 無期徒刑

Every **sentence** has two parts, a subject and a verb.
每個句子都有兩個部分，也就是主詞和動詞。

The English Alphabet

capital letters

small letters

Punctuation Marks

period   comma

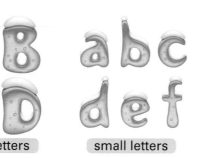

question mark   exclamation mark

pronounce 　發音；發……的音
Learn how to **pronounce** that word correctly. 學習如何正確地發這個字的音。

say 　說
Learn how to **say** that word correctly. 學習如何正確地說這個字。

communicate with 　和……溝通
They learn English to **communicate with** other people.
他們為了和其他人溝通而學英文。

talk to 　和……交談
They learn English to **talk to** other people. 他們為了和其他人交談而學英文。

Word Families ● 099

singular 　單數
A singular word refers to one person, place, or thing.
單數是指單一的人、地或事物。

plural 　複數
A plural word refers to two or more people, places, or things.
複數是指兩個以上的人、地或事物。

uppercase letter 　大寫字母
Use an uppercase letter at the beginning of a sentence.
句首的字母要大寫。

capital letter 　大寫字母
Use a capital letter at the beginning of a sentence.
句首的字母要大寫。

lowercase letter 　小寫字母
Lowercase letters are more common than uppercase letters.
小寫字母比大寫字母更為常見。

small letter 　小寫字母
Small letters are more common than uppercase letters.
小寫字母比大寫字母更為常見。

period 句號 — **Punctuation Marks** 標點符號 — **question mark** 問號

comma 逗號 — **exclamation point** 驚嘆號

Checkup

A

Write | 請依提示寫出正確的英文單字。

1	大寫字母 _____	9	字母；信件 _____
2	小寫字母 _____	10	聲音；音調 _____
3	規則 _____	11	字 _____
4	文法 _____	12	拼字 _____
5	句子 _____	13	書寫；手寫 _____
6	標點符號 _____	14	句號 _____
7	字母表 _____	15	逗號 _____
8	發音 _____	16	和……溝通 _____

B

Complete the Sentences | 請在空格中填入最適當的答案，並視情況做適當的變化。

singular	plural	pronounce	punctuation mark	uppercase letter
small letter	sound	handwriting	communicate with	refer to

1 Learn how to _____ that word correctly. 學習如何正確地發這個字的音。

2 A _____ word refers to one person, place, or thing.
單數是指單一的人、地或事物。

3 Use an _____ _____ at the beginning of a sentence.
句首的字母要大寫。

4 _____ _____ are more common than uppercase letters.
小寫字母比大寫字母更為常見。

5 Nice _____ is easy for people to read. 工整的手寫字體讓人們易於閱讀。

6 _____ _____ like periods and commas are important for writing.
句號、逗號等標點符號在寫作中相當重要。

7 Each letter of the alphabet has its own unique _____.
字母表中的每個字母都有各自獨立的發音。

8 They learn English to _____ _____ other people.
他們為了和其他人溝通而學英文。

C

Read and Choose | 閱讀下列句子，並且選出最適當的答案。

1 There are many (rules | letters) to speaking and writing proper English.

2 A (singular | plural) word refers to two or more people, places, or things.

3 Use a (small | capital) letter at the beginning of a sentence.

4 We use (words | sound) to express our thoughts and feelings.

D

Look, Read, and Write | 看圖並且依照提示，在空格中填入正確答案。

 ▸ a group of words containing a subject and a verb

_____

 ▸ an uppercase letter

_____

 ▸ a lowercase letter

_____

 ▸ the use of symbols such as periods or commas

_____

E

Read and Answer | 閱讀並且回答下列問題。 🔊 100

A Friendly Letter

August 31, 2017

Dear John,

My name is Sara.

I live in Seoul, Korea.
Where do you live?

I go to Central Elementary School.
I like to ride my bike. Please write me back
and tell me about yourself.

Sincerely,

Sara

- **Date:** Begin with the date at the top. Use a capital letter for the name of the month.

- **Greeting:** Start your greeting with "Dear." Use a capital D.

- **Capitalization:** Use capital letters to begin a sentence.

- **Question:** Use question marks at the end of questions.

- **Names:** Capitalize the names of people, places, and things.

- **Closing:** End the letter with a closing and your name.
  Use a capital letter to begin the closing and put a comma after the closing.
  Don't forget that your name should start with a capital letter, too.

Fill in the blanks.

1 A letter should have the _____ at the top.

2 Use question marks at the end of _____.

3 Use a _____ letter for the names of people, places, or things.

4 Write a _____ after the closing.

01 **poem**
['poɪm]

(n.) 詩　*lyric poem 抒情詩　*narrative poem 敘事詩

A **poem** is a short writing that uses rhymes. 詩是指有押韻的短文。

02 **rhyme**
[raɪm]

(n.) 韻；押韻；韻文 (v.) 作押韻詩；作詩　*nursery rhyme 童謠；兒歌

"Like" and "bike" **rhyme** with each other. like 和 bike 互相押韻。

03 **drama**
['drɑmə]

(n.) 戲劇　*costume drama 古裝劇　*drama queen【俚】喜歡小題大做的人

Shakespeare is a famous **drama** writer. 莎士比亞是有名的劇作家。

04 **novel**
['nɑvl̩]

(n.) 小說 (a.) 新奇的　*online/romance/thriller novel 網路／愛情／驚悚小說

A **novel** is a long work of fiction. 小說是指長篇的虛構故事。

05 **folk tale**
[fok tel]

(n.) 民間故事；傳說　= traditional story

Paul Bunyan is a popular American **folk tale**.
《伐木巨人》是有名的美國民間故事。

06 **fairy tale**
['fɛrɪ tel]

(n.) 童話；神話故事　*myth 神話

Hansel and Gretel is a famous **fairy tale** from the Grimm brothers.
《糖果屋》是著名的格林童話故事。

07 **story**
['storɪ]

(n.) 故事；傳聞；傳奇　*the story goes that 傳說……；據說……

Every **story** has a beginning, a middle, and an end.
每個故事都有開始、中間，以及結尾。

08 **fable**
['febl̩]

(n.) 寓言；傳說　*fabled 寓言中的；虛構的

Animals talk and act like people in many of *Aesop's Fables*.
在許多《伊索寓言》的故事中，動物的言行舉止就如同人類一般。

09 **literature**
['lɪtərətʃɚ]

(n.) 文學；文學作品；文獻　*popular literature 大眾文學；通俗文學

Poems, essays, and stories are all kinds of **literature**.
詩、散文和小說都是文學的形式。

10 **character**
['kærɪktɚ]

(n.) 角色；特性；個性　*out of character 不合乎某人的性格

Stories often have several **characters** in them.
故事中通常都有好幾個角色。

Literature

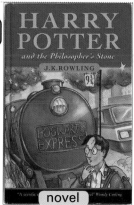

novel

poem

Character

Hansel and Gretel

the witch

Hansel

Gretel

memorize	記住；背熟 Try to memorize your favorite poem. 試著把你最愛的詩背熟。
remember	記得；想起 Try to remember your favorite poem. 試著把你最愛的詩記起來。

pick	挑選；選擇 Pick the fairy tale you want to hear. 選一則你想聽的童話故事。
select	選擇；選拔 Select the fairy tale you want to hear. 選一則你想聽的童話故事。
choose	選擇；決定 Choose the fairy tale you want to hear. 選一則你想聽的童話故事。

read out loud	大聲地唸出來 Moms sometimes read stories out loud to their children. 媽媽有時會大聲地把故事唸給孩子聽。
read aloud	大聲唸 Moms sometimes read stories aloud to their children. 媽媽有時會大聲唸故事給孩子聽。

Word Families ⊙ 103

saying	格言；諺語 A saying is a short sentence that has an important lesson. 格言是一句簡短的重要訓誡。
proverb	諺語；俗諺；常言 A proverb is a short sentence that has an important lesson. 諺語是一句簡短的重要訓誡。

fiction	小說 Works of fiction are made-up stories that are not real. 小說作品是指虛構而非真實的故事。
nonfiction	非小說 Nonfiction works tell true stories or are full of facts. 非小說作品呈現了真實的故事或充滿真實性。

lesson	訓誡；教訓 *The Tortoise and the Hare* has an important lesson in it. 《龜兔賽跑》中有很重要的訓誡。
moral [ˈmɔrəl]	道德規範；寓意 *Aesop's Fables* always had a moral at the end. 《伊索寓言》的結尾總是含有寓意。

Checkup

A

Write | 請依提示寫出正確的英文單字。

1	詩	_____	9	韻；押韻	_____
2	小說	n_____	10	民間故事	_____
3	戲劇	_____	11	記住；背熟	_____
4	童話	_____	12	記得；想起	_____
5	寓言	_____	13	選擇；決定	_____
6	文學	_____	14	故事	_____
7	諺語	_____	15	訓誡；教訓	_____
8	角色	_____	16	非小說	_____

B

Complete the Sentences | 請在空格中填入最適當的答案，並視情況做適當的變化。

novel	fiction	folk tale	fairy tale	poem
fable	moral	rhyme	character	drama

1 Shakespeare is a famous _____ writer. 莎士比亞是有名的劇作家。

2 *Paul Bunyan* is a popular American _____ _____ .《伐木巨人》是有名的美國民間故事。

3 *Hansel and Gretel* is a famous _____ _____ .《糖果屋》是著名的童話故事。

4 _____ is a made-up story that is not real. 小說是指虛構而非真實的故事。

5 Animals talk and act like people in many of *Aesop's* _____ .
在許多《伊索寓言》的故事中，動物的言行舉止就如同人類一般。

6 *Aesop's Fables* always had a _____ at the end.
《伊索寓言》的結尾總是含有寓意。

7 "Like" and "bike" _____ with each other. like 和 bike 互相押韻。

8 Stories often have several _____ in them.
故事中通常都有好幾個角色。

C

Read and Choose | 請選出與鋪底字意思相近的答案。

1 *The Tortoise and the Hare* has an important lesson in it.

   a. fable   b. moral   c. story

2 A saying is a short sentence that has an important lesson.

   a. proverb   b. poem   c. folk tale

3 Pick the fairy tale you want to hear.

   a. Remember   b. Select   c. Read aloud

D Look, Read, and Write | 看圖並且依照提示，在空格中填入正確答案。

 ▸ a person in a book or story

_____

 ▸ a short writing that uses rhymes

_____

 ▸ written stories about people and events that are not real

_____

 ▸ a short sentence that has an important lesson

_____

 ▸ a short story that teaches a moral lesson

_____

 ▸ to choose something or someone

_____

E Read and Answer | 閱讀並且回答下列問題。　104

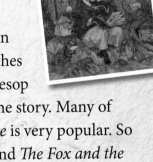

Aesop's Fables

Aesop was a slave who lived in ancient Greece. He lived more than 2,000 years ago. He is famous because of the collection of stories he told. Today, we call them _Aesop's Fables_.

Aesop's Fables are short stories. Often, animals are the main characters. Through the stories about animals, Aesop teaches us how we should act as people. At the end of the fable, Aesop always tells us a lesson. The lesson is called the moral of the story. Many of his stories are still famous today. _The Tortoise and the Hare_ is very popular. So is _The Ant and the Grasshopper_. _The Lion and the Mouse_ and _The Fox and the Grapes_ are also well known.

What is true? Write T (true) or F (false).

1   Aesop was an ancient Greek king.　　　_____

2   _Aesop's Fables_ are very long stories.　　　_____

3   The characters in _Aesop's Fables_ are often animals.　　　_____

4   _The Ant and the Mouse_ is a famous story from _Aesop's Fables_.

A World of Lines and Colors

線與色彩的世界

Key Words 🔊 105

01	**color**	(n.) 顏色 (v.) 著色　*color-blind 色盲的
	[ˋkʌlɚ]	Red, yellow, and blue are called the primary colors. 紅色、黃色和藍色稱為三原色。

02	**line**	(n.) 線;隊伍　*dotted line 虛線
	[laɪn]	There are many types of lines, such as straight, curved, and spiral. 線有許多種,如直線、曲線和螺線。

03	**shape**	(n.) 形狀　*in the shape of 呈……的形狀
	[ʃep]	Three common shapes are the circle, square, and triangle. 圓形、正方形和三角形是常見的三種形狀。

04	**texture**	(n.) 質地;組織;結構　*rough texture 質地粗糙
	[ˋtɛkstʃɚ]	The texture of the fur is very soft. 軟毛的質地非常柔軟。

05	**painting**	(n.) 繪畫;畫作　*abstract painting 抽象畫
	[ˋpentɪŋ]	One of the most famous paintings in the world is the *Mona Lisa*. 《蒙娜麗莎》是世界名畫之一。

06	**drawing**	(n.) 描繪;圖畫　*drawing board 製圖版;畫圖版
	[ˋdrɔɪŋ]	Artists use pens and charcoal to make drawings. 藝術家用筆和木炭作畫。

07	**sculpture**	(n.) 雕刻品;雕像 (v.) 雕刻　= carve
	[ˋskʌlptʃɚ]	Sculptures can be made of stone, wood, or metal. 石頭、木頭或金屬都可以做成雕刻品。

08	**portrait**	(n.) 肖像;半身的雕塑像;描繪　*self-portrait 自畫像
	[ˋportret]	A portrait is a picture of a person. 肖像是指一個人的畫像。

09	**mural**	(n.) 壁畫;壁飾　*muralist 壁畫家
	[ˋmjʊrəl]	A mural is a large painting done on a wall. 壁畫是指在牆上完成的巨畫。

10	**statue**	(n.) 雕像
	[ˋstætʃu]	The Statue of Liberty is made of copper. 自由女神像是由銅製成的。

painting　　drawing　　sculpture　　mural

paint	繪畫;油漆 Picasso painted many beautiful pictures. 畢卡索畫了許多美麗的畫。
draw	繪製;描寫 Picasso drew many beautiful pictures. 畢卡索繪製了許多美麗的畫。
make	製造;建造;做 The sculptor is making a statue. 雕刻家正在製作雕像。
create	創造;創作;設計 The sculptor is creating a statue. 雕刻家正在創造雕像。
mix colors	把顏色混合;調色 You can mix colors together to create different ones. 你可以把顏色混在一起創造出另一個顏色。
make colors	調色 You can make colors like orange by mixing red and yellow. 把紅色和黃色混合,你就可以調出像橘色的顏色。

Word Families 🔊 107

painter	畫家 A painter uses paint to create pictures. 畫家用顏料畫畫。
sculptor	雕刻家 A sculptor uses stone, wood, or metal to make statues. 雕刻家用石頭、木頭或金屬製作雕像。
artist	藝術家 An artist may draw, paint pictures, or sculpt. 藝術家是指繪製、描繪圖畫或雕像的人。

Lines
線

straight line
直線

curved line
曲線

zigzag line
鋸齒線;Z 字型線

spiral line
螺線

fine line
細線

rough line
粗線

Checkup

Write | 請依提示寫出正確的英文單字。

1 形狀	_____	9 繪畫;油漆	_____
2 質地	_____	10 創造;創作	_____
3 繪畫;畫作	_____	11 調色	_____
4 雕刻品	_____	12 直線	_____
5 肖像	_____	13 曲線	_____
6 壁畫	_____	14 雕刻家	_____
7 雕像	_____	15 畫家	_____
8 描繪;圖畫	_____	16 藝術家	_____

B

Complete the Sentences | 請在空格中填入最適當的答案,並視情況做適當的變化。

paint	portrait	painter	make colors	artist
statue	make	sculptor	primary color	line

1 Red, yellow, and blue are called the _____ _____.
   紅色、黃色和藍色稱為三原色。

2 Picasso _____ many beautiful pictures. 畢卡索畫了許多美麗的畫。

3 You can _____ _____ like green by mixing blue and yellow.
   把藍色和黃色混合,你就可以調出像綠色的顏色。

4 A _____ is an artist who paints pictures. 描繪圖畫的藝術家稱為畫家。

5 A _____ uses stone, wood, or metal to make statues.
   雕刻家用石頭、木頭或金屬製作雕像。

6 The _____ of Liberty is made of copper. 自由女神像是由銅製成的。

7 An _____ may draw, paint pictures, or sculpt.
   藝術家是指繪製、描繪圖畫或雕像的人。

8 The sculptor is _____ a statue. 雕刻家正在製作雕像。

C

Read and Choose | 閱讀下列句子,並且選出最適當的答案。

1 One of the most famous (sculptures | paintings) in the world is the *Mona Lisa*.

2 You can (mix colors | make colors) together to get different ones.

3 Three common (shapes | lines) are the circle, square, and triangle.

4 There are many types of (shapes | lines), such as straight, curved, and spiral.

Look, Read, and Write | 看圖並且依照提示，在空格中填入正確答案。

1  ▶ to combine colors

_____

4  ▶ a picture of a person

_____

2 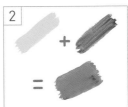 ▶ yellow + blue =

_____

5  ▶ a large painting done on a wall

_____

3  ▶ three primary colors

_____

6  ▶ a picture made with pencil or charcoal

_____

Read and Answer | 閱讀並且回答下列問題。 ● 108

Primary and Secondary Colors

There are three basic colors. They are red, yellow, and blue. We call these three primary colors. You can make other colors when you mix these colors together. For example, mix red and yellow to create orange. Combine yellow and blue to make green. And you get purple or violet when you mix red and blue together. We call these secondary colors.

Of course, there are many other colors. You can make black by mixing red, yellow, and blue all together. You can also mix primary and secondary colors to get other colors.

Fill in the blanks.

1   Red, _____, and blue are three primary colors.

2   Green, orange, and purple are _____ colors.

3   Combine red and blue to get _____.

4   _____ is a combination of red, yellow, and blue.

Unit 28 A World of Paintings 繪畫的世界

Key Words ⊙ 109

01 **brushstroke**
['brʌʃstrok]

(n.) 筆法；一筆；一畫

It takes many **brushstrokes** to complete a painting.
完成一幅畫需要有許多筆法。

02 **touch**
[tʌtʃ]

(n.) 筆觸；觸感 (v.) 接觸；觸摸　　*keep in touch 保持聯繫　　*a touch of 少許

An artist needs a good **touch** to make a painting.
藝術家要有優美的筆觸才能夠繪製一幅畫。

03 **tone**
[ton]

(n.) 色調；聲調；語氣　　*color tone 色調

Some painters like dark **tones**. 有些畫家喜歡陰鬱的色調。

04 **object**
['ɑbdʒɪkt]

(n.) 物體；對象；目標　　*inanimate object 靜物

The artist must first choose the **object** that he will paint.
藝術家必須先選擇要描繪的物體。

05 **still life**
[stɪl laɪf]

(n.) 靜物寫生；靜物畫　　*an exhibit of still lifes 靜物展覽

A **still life** is a picture of flowers, fruit, or other small objects that do not
move. 靜物畫是指畫中有花、水果或其他不會移動的小型物體。

06 **landscape**
['lænd,skep]

(n.) 景色；風景；風景畫　　*landscape architecture 造景建築藝術

A **landscape** is a painting of an outside place, such as trees, mountains and
rivers. 風景畫是指描繪戶外地點的畫，像是樹木、山和河流。

07 **arrange**
[ə'rendʒ]

(v.) 安排；佈置　　*arrange for 為……作安排

The artist must first **arrange** the objects that will be in the painting.
藝術家必須要先佈置物體在畫中的位置。

08 **trace**
[tres]

(v.) 描摹；摹寫；追蹤　　(cf.) tracing paper 描圖紙；摹圖紙　　*trace back 追溯

You can **trace** a picture by placing tracing paper over it.
你可以藉由在上面放置一張描圖紙描摹一幅畫。

09 **sketch**
[skɛtʃ]

(n.) 素描；草圖；概略 (v.) 素描；速寫　　*sketch pad 速寫簿；寫生簿

Some artists make a **sketch** by drawing a picture very quickly.
有些藝術家畫一幅素描的速度很快。

10 **sculpt**
[skʌlpt]

(v.) 雕刻；造型　　= carve

Sculptors usually **sculpt** with stone or clay. 雕刻家通常會用石頭或黏土來雕刻。

landscape

still life

sketch

sculpt

observe　看到；觀察
The artist must first observe the scene he will paint.
藝術家必須先觀察要描繪的風景。

look at　看
The artist must first look at the scene he will paint.
藝術家必須先看要描繪的風景。

be drawn by　由……所繪製的
The picture was drawn by Picasso. 這幅畫是由畢卡索所繪製的。

be painted by　由……畫的
The painting was painted by Manet. 這幅畫是馬奈畫的。

be made by　由……所製成的
The statue was made by Rodin. 這座雕像是由羅丹所刻製而成的。

Word Families 🔊 111

watercolor　水彩；水彩顏料
Watercolor pictures are often very bright. 水彩畫通常都非常明亮。

oils　油畫；油畫顏料
Oils are popular with a large number of painters. 許多畫家都喜歡畫油畫。

crayon　蠟筆；蠟筆畫
Children frequently make pictures with crayons. 小孩子常會用蠟筆畫畫。

brush　畫筆；毛筆
An artist applies paint with a brush. 藝術家用畫筆沾上顏料。

easel　畫架
[ˈizl]
Artists put their pictures on easels while they paint them.
藝術家作畫時會把畫放置在畫架上。

canvas　帆布；油畫布
[ˈkænvəs]
Most pictures are painted on canvas. 大部分的畫都畫在帆布上。

colored pencil 色鉛筆	marker 麥克筆

| watercolor 水彩顏料 | **Drawing Materials** 繪圖材料 | colored chalk 彩色粉筆 |

| paints 顏料 | crayon 蠟筆 |

Checkup

A Write | 請依提示寫出正確的英文單字。

1	靜物畫	_____	9	筆觸；觸感	_____
2	風景畫	_____	10	色調；聲調	_____
3	筆法	_____	11	物體；對象	_____
4	描摹；摹寫	_____	12	水彩	_____
5	雕刻	_____	13	油畫	_____
6	安排	_____	14	顏料	_____
7	看	_____	15	畫架	_____
8	素描	_____	16	帆布	_____

B

Complete the Sentences | 請在空格中填入最適當的答案，並視情況做適當的變化。

arrange	brushstroke	tone	make	easel
draw	tracing paper	touch	canvas	oils

1 It takes many _____ to complete a painting.
完成一幅畫需要有許多筆法。

2 The statue was _____ by Rodin. 這座雕像是由羅丹所刻製而成的。

3 The picture was _____ by Manet. 這幅畫是馬奈畫的。

4 The artist must first _____ the objects that will be in the painting.
藝術家必須要先佈置物體在畫中的位置。

5 _____ are popular with a large number of painters. 許多畫家都喜歡畫油畫。

6 Some painters prefer dark _____. 有些畫家喜歡陰鬱的色調。

7 You can trace a picture by placing _____ _____ over it.
你可以藉由在上面放置一張描圖紙描摹一幅畫。

8 An artist needs a good _____ to make a painting.
藝術家要有優美的筆觸才能夠繪製一幅畫。

C

Read and Choose | 閱讀下列句子，並且選出最適當的答案。

1 (Oil paints | Watercolor pictures) are often very bright.

2 Sculptors usually (sculpt | draw) with stone or clay.

3 Most pictures are painted on (easel | canvas).

D   Look, Read, and Write ┃ 看圖並且依照提示，在空格中填入正確答案。

 ▶ a painting of an outside place

_____

 ▶ a picture of flowers or fruits that do not move

_____

 ▶ an object with short pieces of stiff hair, used for painting

_____

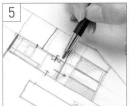 ▶ a stick of colored wax used for drawing

_____

 ▶ a quick, rough drawing that shows the main features of an object

_____

 ▶ to look at something carefully

_____

E

Read and Answer ┃ 閱讀並且回答下列問題。 112

Famous Painters

Art galleries display the works of lots of painters. There have been many painters. Some of them are very famous. Artists make many different kinds of paintings. But they are all beautiful in their own way.

Picasso was a famous modern painter. Manet, Monet, Cezanne, and van Gogh painted more than 100 years ago. Leonardo da Vinci was very famous also. He painted the most famous portrait in the world: the *Mona Lisa*. Rembrandt was a painter from a long time ago. So was Michelangelo. He painted around 500 years ago.

Answer the questions.

1   Where can you see the works of painters?   _____

2   Who was a famous modern painter?   _____

3   Who painted the *Mona Lisa*?   _____

4   How long ago did Michelangelo paint?   _____

Unit 29 Instruments and Their Families

01 **instrument**
[ˈɪnstrəmənt]

(n.) 樂器；儀器；器具　　*stringed instrument 弦樂器

There are many kinds of musical **instruments**. 樂器有許多種類。

02 **piano**
[pɪˈæno]

(n.) 鋼琴　　*electric piano 電子琴

The **piano** uses a keyboard to make sounds.
鋼琴利用鍵盤來發出聲音。

03 **violin**
[ˌvaɪəˈlɪn]

(n.) 小提琴　　*cello 大提琴

The **violin** has four strings, and you play it with a bow.
小提琴共有四條弦，可用琴弓演奏。

04 **drum**
[drʌm]

(n.) 鼓　　*play the drums 打鼓

The **drum**, xylophone, and cymbals are in the same family.
鼓、木琴和鈸都屬於同一類的樂器。

05 **flute**
[flut]

(n.) 長笛　　*fluting 吹長笛；長笛般的聲音

You play the **flute** and clarinet by blowing air on them.
長笛和豎笛都是用吹奏的。

06 **trumpet**
[ˈtrʌmpɪt]

(n.) 喇叭；擴音器 *(v.)* 吹喇叭；大聲疾呼

The **trumpet** is made of a shiny metal called brass.
喇叭是由一種稱為黃銅的亮面金屬材質所製成的。

07 **orchestra**
[ˈɔrkɪstrə]

(n.) 管弦樂隊；管弦樂器　　*symphony orchestra 交響樂團

All types of instruments come together in an **orchestra** to make beautiful
music. 所有種類的管絃樂器結合在一起製造出美麗的音樂。

08 **band**
[bænd]

(n.) 樂團；帶子　　*brass band 銅管樂隊

Most **bands** have both musicians and singers in them.
大部分的樂團裡頭都有樂師和歌手。

09 **composer**
[kəmˈpozɚ]

(n.) 作曲家　　= melodist

Beethoven and Mozart were famous **composers** of classical music.
貝多芬和莫札特都是有名的古典樂派作曲家。

10 **conductor**
[kənˈdʌktɚ]

(n.) 指揮；領導者；車掌

A **conductor** leads an orchestra. 指揮領導著一支管絃樂隊。

Orchestra

musician

conductor

play	演奏;彈奏;表演 The band will **play** this Friday night. 樂團會在這星期五晚上表演。
perform	演出;表演 The band will **perform** this Friday night. 樂團會在這星期五晚上演出。
compose	作曲;組成 Some musicians **compose** their own songs. 有些音樂家會自己作曲。
write	寫;編寫(樂曲) Some musicians **write** their own songs. 有些音樂家會自己編曲。
conduct	指揮(樂隊、軍隊等) Beethoven used to **conduct** the orchestra himself. 貝多芬曾經親自指揮管絃樂團。
direct	指揮;指導 Beethoven used to **direct** the orchestra himself. 貝多芬曾經親自指揮管絃樂團。
read music	閱讀樂譜 (= read sheet music) A musician must be able to **read music**. 音樂家一定要會看樂譜。
read musical notes	閱讀樂譜;閱讀音符 A musician must be able to **read musical notes**. 音樂家一定要看得懂音符。

Word Families 🔘 115

Piano
鋼琴

- **piano music** 鋼琴樂
- **piano concert** 鋼琴演奏會
- **piano lesson** 鋼琴課
- **piano solo** 鋼琴獨奏
- **piano duet** 鋼琴二重奏
- **piano trio** 鋼琴三重奏

Musicians
音樂家

- **pianist** 鋼琴家
- **violinist** 小提琴家
- **guitarist** 吉他手
- **drummer** 鼓手
- **flutist** 長笛吹奏者
- **trumpeter** 小號手

orchestra instruments

Checkup

A

Write | 請依提示寫出正確的英文單字。

1	樂器	_____	
2	管弦樂隊	_____	
3	作曲家	_____	
4	指揮	_____	
5	音樂家	_____	
6	表演	_____	
7	作曲	_____	
8	閱讀樂譜	_____	

9	演奏樂器	_____
10	鋼琴獨奏	_____
11	鋼琴二重奏	_____
12	鋼琴家	_____
13	吉他手	_____
14	小提琴家	_____
15	鼓手	_____
16	小號手	_____

B

Complete the Sentences | 請在空格中填入最適當的答案，並視情況做適當的變化。

conduct	composer	play	read music	write
singer	orchestra	band	musical instrument	blow

1   All types of instruments come together in an _____.
    所有種類的管絃樂器結合在一起製造出美麗的音樂。

2   A musician must be able to _____ _____. 音樂家一定要會看樂譜。

3   The band will _____ this Friday night. 樂團會在這星期五晚上表演。

4   Beethoven used to _____ the orchestra himself.
    貝多芬曾經親自指揮管絃樂團。

5   Some musicians _____ their own songs. 有些音樂家會自己編曲。

6   Beethoven and Mozart were famous _____.
    貝多芬和莫札特都是有名的作曲家。

7   There are many kinds of _____ _____.
    樂器有許多種類。

8   Most bands have both musicians and _____ in them.
    大部分的樂團裡頭都有樂師和歌手。

C

Read and Choose | 閱讀下列句子，並且選出最適當的答案。

1   The piano uses (keyboards | strings) to make sounds.

2   The (trumpet | violin) has four strings.

3   The (trumpet | xylophone) and trombone are made of brass.

4   You play the (flute | drum) and clarinet by blowing air on them.

D Look, Read, and Write | 看圖並且依照提示，在空格中填入正確答案。

 ▶ a person who directs
an orchestra

_____

 ▶ to perform on a
musical instrument

_____

 ▶ a person who writes
music

_____

 ▶ to write music

_____

 ▶ a person who plays
a musical instrument

_____

 ▶ a group of musicians
using many different
instruments to play
mostly classical
music

_____

E Read and Answer | 閱讀並且回答下列問題。 ⊙ 116

Musicians and Their Musical Instruments

There are so many kinds of musical instruments.
They make many different sounds. So there are also
many kinds of music. Rock musicians often use
the guitar and drums. Jazz music needs a piano and
saxophone. And classical music uses many various kinds of instruments.

People often play two or more instruments together. They do this in a band or
an orchestra. But the musicians must all play at the same time. Many of them
read sheet music. This tells them what notes to play. If they play well together,
they create a harmonious sound.

What is true? Write T (true) or F (false).

1   Jazz musicians often play the piano.   _____

2   The drums are common in rock music.   _____

3   A band only needs one musical instrument.   _____

4   Musicians read music to learn what instrument to play.   _____

A World of Music 音樂世界

Key Words 🔘 117

01	**words** [wɝdz]	(n.) 詞；單字　*play on words 雙關語 Some musicians write the words to their own songs. 有些音樂家會為自創歌曲填詞。
02	**tune** [tjun]	(n.) 曲調 (v.) 調……的音或頻道　*out of tune with 音高或調子不正確 A real singer can carry a tune. 真正的歌手能夠唱出曲調。
03	**melody** [ˈmɛlədɪ]	(n.) 旋律；歌曲　*beautiful melodies 優美的旋律 This song has a good melody. 這首歌的旋律很美。
04	**harmony** [ˈhɑrmənɪ]	(n.) 和諧；和睦；融洽　*in harmony with 與……協調一致 When sounds match or go together, they make a harmony. 聲音相配就會產生和諧的感覺。
05	**rhythm** [ˈrɪðəm]	(n.) 節奏；韻律；律動　*sense of rhythm 節奏感 Popular songs usually have a good rhythm. 受歡迎的歌曲通常都有很優美的節奏。
06	**beat** [bit]	(n.) 拍子；節奏 (n.) 擊；打 *beat time to sth.（按照音樂節奏，用揮棍或踏腳等方式）打拍子 A big part of rhythm is called beat. 節奏中最重要的部分稱為拍子。
07	**hum** [hʌm]	(v.) 哼曲子；蜜蜂嗡嗡叫　*the hum of bees 蜜蜂的嗡嗡聲 Some people enjoy humming their favorite songs. 有些人喜歡哼自己最愛的歌曲。
08	**keep time** [kip taɪm]	(v.) 合拍子 (= keep the beat) Try to keep time so that you don't lose your place in the song. 要努力合拍子才不會跟不上這首歌。
09	**opera** [ˈɑpərə]	(n.) 歌劇　*opera house 歌劇院；劇場 Operas tell stories by using songs. 歌劇藉由歌曲來詮釋故事。
10	**ballet** [ˈbæle]	(n.) 芭蕾舞；芭蕾舞曲；芭蕾舞團 Ballets rely upon music and dancing to tell a story. 芭蕾舞透過音樂和舞蹈來詮釋故事。

audience / performer

band / lead singer

opera singer

ballet dancer

⊙ 118

make a sound　製造聲音
Musical instruments can **make** a variety of **sounds**. 樂器能夠製造出多種聲音。

create a sound　製造聲音；引起聲音
Musical instruments can **create** a variety of **sounds**. 樂器能夠製造出多種聲音。

match　和諧；和……相配
The two singers' voices **match** well. 這兩位歌手的聲音很和諧。

go together　相配
The two singers' voices **go together** well. 這兩位歌手的聲音很相配。

write music　作曲
Mozart was very good at **writing music**. 莫札特很會作曲。

read music　閱讀樂譜
A good musician must be able to **read music**.
一位優秀的音樂家必須要看得懂樂譜。

play music　奏出音樂
The band can **play** good **music**. 這個樂團能夠演奏出優美的音樂。

Word Families ⊙ 119

singer　歌手
She is the lead **singer** for a band. 她是這個樂團的主唱。

performer　演奏者；表演者
The **performer** enjoys playing in front of audiences.
演奏者喜歡在觀眾面前表演。

audience　觀眾；聽眾
The **audience** clapped at the end of the performance. 觀眾在表演結束後拍手鼓掌。

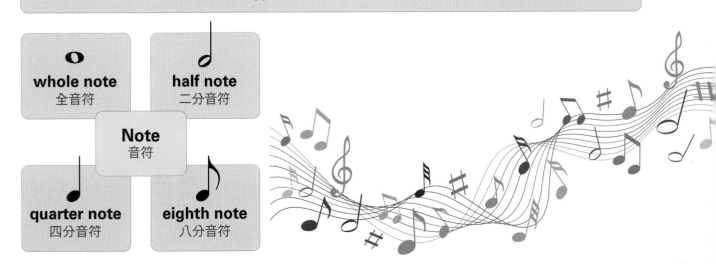

whole note 全音符	**half note** 二分音符
Note 音符	
quarter note 四分音符	**eighth note** 八分音符

Checkup

A

Write | 請依提示寫出正確的英文單字。

1	旋律	_____	9	觀眾;聽眾 _____
2	詞	_____	10	全音符 _____
3	曲調	_____	11	二分音符 _____
4	和諧	_____	12	閱讀樂譜 _____
5	節奏;韻律	_____	13	演奏者;表演者 _____
6	拍子	_____	14	哼曲子;蜜蜂嗡嗡叫 _____
7	歌劇	_____	15	合拍子 _____
8	芭蕾舞	_____	16	奏出音樂 _____

B

Complete the Sentences | 請在空格中填入最適當的答案,並視情況做適當的變化。

make	harmony	keep time	words	audience	rhythm

1 Popular songs usually have a good _____.
受歡迎的歌曲通常都有很優美的節奏。

2 When sounds match or go together, they make a _____.
聲音相配就會產生和諧的感覺。

3 Musical instruments can _____ a variety of sounds. 樂器能夠製造出多種聲音。

4 Some musicians write the _____ to their own songs.
有些音樂家會為自創歌曲填詞。

5 You should _____ _____ so that you don't lose your place in the song.
你應該要合拍子才不會跟不上這首歌。

6 The _____ clapped at the end of the performance.
觀眾在表演結束後拍手鼓掌。

C

Read and Choose | 請選出與鋪底字意思相近的答案。

1 A real singer can carry a tune.
   a. beat   b. melody   c. word

2 The two singers' voices match well.
   a. go together   b. hum   c. perform

3 Mozart was very good at writing music.
   a. making sounds   b. composing   c. reading music

4 The musician enjoys playing in front of audiences.
   a. singing   b. humming   c. performing

D

Look, Read, and Write | 看圖並且依照提示，在空格中填入正確答案。

 ▶ a person who sings

_____

 ▶ a person who plays in front of audiences

_____

 ▶ the people watching or listening to a concert

_____

 ▶ an individual sound in music

_____

 ▶ a play using songs to tell a story

_____

 ▶ a type of dancing using music to tell a story

_____

E

Read and Answer | 閱讀並且回答下列問題。 120

Popular Children's Songs

What makes a song popular? There are many factors involved. Often, the simplest songs are the most popular with people. The words to the song might be easy, so people can remember them easily. Or the melody is easy to play or remember, so people often hum or whistle the music.

Some songs are well-liked by young people. *Bingo* is one of these songs. *Old MacDonald* is another, and so are *Twinkle, Twinkle, Little Star* and *La Cucaracha*. Why do people like them? The words often repeat, the words rhyme, and the tunes are catchy.

Fill in the blanks.

1   Many times, _____ songs are popular.

2   Some people like to _____ or whistle music.

3   *Twinkle, Twinkle, Little* _____ is a song young people like.

4   Popular songs often have _____ tunes.

A

Write | 請依提示寫出正確的英文單字。

1	文法	_____	11	繪畫;油漆	_____
2	句子	_____	12	肖像	_____
3	繪畫;畫作	_____	13	觀眾;聽眾	_____
4	雕刻品;雕像	_____	14	古典音樂	_____
5	樂器	_____	15	合拍子	_____
6	管弦樂隊	_____	16	奏出音樂	_____
7	作曲家	_____	17	記住;背熟	_____
8	表演	_____	18	選擇;決定	_____
9	作曲	_____	19	大聲念	_____
10	閱讀樂譜	_____	20	小說	f_____

B

Choose the Correct Word | 請選出與鋪底字意思相近的答案。

1 A real singer can carry a tune.

   a. beat   b. melody   c. word

2 The two singers' voices match well.

   a. go together   b. hum   c. perform

3 *The Tortoise and the Hare* has an important lesson in it.

   a. fable   b. moral   c. story

4 A saying is a short sentence that has an important lesson.

   a. proverb   b. poem   c. folk tale

C

Complete the Sentences | 請在空格中填入最適當的答案,並視情況做適當的變化。

orchestra	drama	draw	rhythm

1 Shakespeare is a famous _____ writer. 莎士比亞是有名的劇作家。

2 The picture was _____ by Picasso. 這幅畫是由畢卡索所繪製的。

3 All types of instruments come together in an _____.
所有種類的管弦樂器結合在一起製造出美麗的音樂。

4 Popular songs usually have a good _____.
受歡迎的歌曲通常都有很優美的節奏。

Index

143

ANSWERS
AND
TRANSLATIONS

01 ● Our Community (p. 12)

A

1 neighborhood   2 community   3 city   4 suburb
5 leader   6 state   7 country   8 citizen
9 post office   10 citizenship   11 take   12 ride on
13 reside   14 get to know   15 avenue
16 transportation

B

1 neighborhood   2 citizen   3 leader
4 Citizenship   5 get along   6 take
7 community center   8 countries

C

1 Suburbs   2 city   3 states   4 reside

D

1 neighborhood, community   2 suburbs   3 city
4 leader   5 community center   6 citizen

E 好鄰居

　　你的鄰居就是住在你家附近的人。在我們的社區裡，人們會互相幫忙、彼此照應。若是想要有個好鄰居，你必須先成為一個好鄰居。要做到這點有很多方法。首先，你可以對鄰居表示友好。要經常和他們打招呼，並且說「你好」。去認識他們，和他們成為朋友。還有，不要在家裡製造噪音，並且要尊重鄰居的隱私。他們若是遇到問題，你可以幫助他們，將來他們也會幫助你的。如果這些你都做到了，你就是個好鄰居。

*** care about** 關心；在乎；介意　**greet** 問候
　privacy 隱私；私生活

填空
1 鄰居就是住在你家附近的人。(Neighbors)
2 你應該要對鄰居表示友好。(nice)
3 要試著尊重鄰居的隱私。(privacy)
4 好鄰居通常會幫助其他鄰居。(help)

02 ● Home and School Life (p. 16)

A

1 manners   2 behavior   3 rule   4 class
5 hallway   6 activity   7 playground   8 recess
9 homeroom   10 get along   11 listen
12 recite   13 state   14 follow   15 pay attention
16 Pledge of Allegiance

B

1 rules   2 behavior   3 class   4 manners
5 playground   6 recess   7 activities
8 homeroom

C

1 (b)   2 (a)   3 (c)

D

1 Raise   2 cheat   3 quiet   4 outside   5 Listen
6 Get along

E 在學校的一天

　　約翰和莎莉在上小學。他們的第一堂課從早上 8 點開始。他們到大教室去。在開始上課之前，他們會立正、面向國旗，並且說出「忠誠宣誓」，之後他們的老師史密斯太太才會開始上課。他們上了數學課、社會課、英文課和美術課，然後到自助餐廳吃午餐。中餐過後是他們的休息時間，所以全體學生都會到戶外玩。他們還上了自然課、歷史課和音樂課。最後到了三點鐘，就是他們該回家的時候了！

*** face** 面向；朝；向

以下何者為「是」？請在空格中填入「T」或「F」。
1 約翰和莎莉的第一堂課從 9 點開始。(F)
2 約翰和莎莉的級任老師是史密斯太太。(T)
3 約翰和莎莉的數學課和美術課在午餐以前。(T)
4 約翰和莎莉的自然課和社會課在午餐以後。(F)

03 ● Different Cultures and Holidays (p. 20)

A

1 culture   2 holiday   3 custom   4 tradition
5 pride   6 ancestor   7 ceremony   8 favorite
9 respect   10 honor   11 give   12 receive
13 remember   14 recall   15 celebrate   16 hold

B

1 culture   2 customs   3 favorite   4 ancestors
5 ceremony   6 pride   7 remember   8 tradition

C

1 celebrate   2 give   3 honors   4 respect

D

1 Christmas   2 New Year's Day   3 Easter
4 Valentine's Day   5 Independence Day
6 Thanksgiving Day

E 習俗和文化的差異

　　美國人有自己的習俗和文化，但許多國家也有習俗和文化。我們應該認識其他人的習俗和文化，並且尊重它們。舉例來說，美國人在家會穿鞋子，但在日本和韓國等亞洲國家，人們進入住家前會先脫鞋。還有，美國人用餐時使用刀叉，但在印度等其他國家，人們是用雙手。還有許多其他差異，這些是我們都應該知道且多加認識的。

填空
1 每個國家有自己的習俗和文化。(cultures)
2 美國人在家會穿鞋子。(shoes)
3 美國人用餐時使用刀叉。(eat)
4 印度人通常用雙手吃飯。(India)

04 • The American Government (p. 24)

A

1 capital 2 citizen 3 election 4 vote 5 law
6 right 7 freedom 8 government 9 symbol
10 flag 11 elect 12 government officials
13 protect 14 defend 15 govern 16 symbolize

B

1 citizens 2 capital 3 rights 4 freedom
5 Laws 6 government 7 elect 8 elections

C

1 (c) 2 (a) 3 (a)

D

1 the Statue of Liberty 2 the American flag
3 mayor 4 the Capitol Building
5 the bald eagle 6 Washington, D.C.

E 美國政府的領導人

　　總統是美國政府的領導人。他是由人民所選出來的，任期為四年，住在白宮。還有其他政府官員，多數人都任職於國會。國會分成兩個部分，也就是參議院和眾議院。每個州都有兩位參議員，每州的眾議員數則不一。有些州有好幾位，但有的只有一、兩位。國會議員制定了全國法律，他們工作的地點在華盛頓特區裡的國會大廈。

＊**serve** 任職　**Congress** 美國國會
　the Senate 美國參議院　**senator** 參議員
　the House of Representatives 眾議院
　representative 眾議員

閱讀並且回答下列問題。
1 美國政府的領導人為何人？(the president)
2 總統住在哪裡？(the White House)
3 每個州各有幾位參議員？(two)
4 美國國會位於何處？(the Capitol in Washington, D.C.)

05 • World Religions (p. 28)

A

1 religion 2 Christianity 3 Judaism 4 Islam
5 Buddhism 6 Hinduism 7 holy book 8 belief
9 prayer 10 priest 11 Buddhist 12 pray
13 worship 14 follow 15 follower 16 spread

B

1 religions 2 follow 3 Hinduism's 4 prayer
5 belief 6 believe in 7 pray 8 spread

C

1 Christianity 2 Islam 3 Buddhism
4 holy books

D

1 Christians 2 Jews 3 Muslims 4 Buddhists
5 Hindus 6 religion

E 基督教的節日

　　基督教徒就是信仰基督教的人。他們相信耶穌基督是上帝的兒子。基督教有兩個非常重要的節日，也就是聖誕節和復活節。聖誕節是在 12 月 25 日，基督徒會在這天慶祝耶穌的誕生。聖誕節是一段充滿歡樂和慶祝的時光。復活節是在每年的三月底或四月初，它是基督教最重要的節日。這一天是耶穌基督死而復活的日子。大部分的基督徒這天都會上教堂。

＊**celebrate** 慶祝　**celebration** 慶祝活動

以下何者為非？(2)
1 基督教徒相信耶穌基督是上帝的兒子。
2 復活節是在 12 月 25 日。
3 耶穌是在聖誕節出生。
4 復活節是基督教最重要的節日。

Review Test **1**

A

1 neighborhood 2 community 3 manners
4 behavior 5 rule 6 culture 7 holiday
8 freedom 9 government 10 religion
11 neighbor 12 citizen 13 get along
14 respect 15 honor 16 elect
17 vote 18 Christianity 19 Judaism 20 Islam

B

1 (c) 2 (c) 3 (a) 4 (a)

C

1 Citizenship 2 culture 3 believe in 4 rules

06 • Our Land and Water (p. 34)

A

1 river 2 lake 3 stream 4 forest 5 plain
6 desert 7 mountain 8 hill 9 ocean 10 island
11 be surrounded by 12 be made up of 13 climb
14 walk through 15 sail on 16 coast

B

1 rivers 2 deserts 3 ocean 4 mountain
5 lake 6 stream 7 Hills 8 beaches

C

1 surrounded by 2 hiking 3 sailing
4 made up of

D

1 lake 2 mountain 3 island 4 ocean 5 forest
6 desert

E 國家公園

　　美國有許多座國家公園，這些地方都是保育區。因此，人們不可以開發或破壞它們。

　　第一座國家公園是黃石國家公園。它是一個風光明媚的地方，還有許多野生動物。大峽谷也是一座國家公園，它是全世界最廣大的峽谷之一。每年有上百萬人造訪這些公園。他們會參觀公園和健行，有些人甚至會在公園裡露營。他們也認識了關於這塊土地的故事，還有要如何保護它。

* stunning 極漂亮的；令人震驚的 **scenery** 風景；景色
canyon 峽谷

閱讀並且回答下列問題。
1 哪一個國家有很多座國家公園？
　(the United States)
2 第一座國家公園叫什麼名字？
　(Yellowstone National Park)
3 全世界最廣大的峽谷之一叫作什麼名字？
　(the Grand Canyon)
4 人們在國家公園裡會從事何種活動？
　(tour, go hiking, and camp)

07 Unit ● Oceans and Continents (p. 38)

A
1 Asia　2 Europe　3 Africa　4 Australia
5 North America　6 South America　7 Antarctica
8 Pacific Ocean　9 Atlantic Ocean
10 Indian Ocean　11 be next to
12 be located/situated in　13 land　14 bay
15 gulf　16 peninsula
B
1 Asia　2 Europe　3 South America　4 located
5 Africa　6 land　7 Pacific Ocean　8 continents
C
1 North America　2 water　3 is next to　4 ocean
D
1 island　2 Asia　3 Australia　4 Pacific Ocean
5 Atlantic Ocean　6 Indian Ocean

E 海洋和大陸
　　世界有七大洲，其中亞洲的面積最大。許多國家都位於歐洲，而沙漠和叢林都在非洲。亞洲、歐洲和非洲一般稱為「舊世界」。澳洲則是全世界最大的島。人們稱北美洲和南美洲為「新世界」。
　　世界有五大海洋，其中以太平洋的面積最大。大西洋位於舊世界與新世界之間。印度洋是唯一以國家名稱命名的海洋。北極海和南極海都非常寒冷。
* named for 以……命名

以下何者為非？(3)
1 亞洲是舊世界的一部分。
2 澳洲是一塊很大的島嶼。
3 世界有七大海洋。
4 太平洋的面積較大西洋大。

08 Unit ● Maps and Directions (p. 42)

A
1 map　2 symbol　3 map key　4 compass
5 location　6 direction　7 intersection　8 turn
9 route　10 instructions　11 mean　12 symbolize
13 west　14 be located　15 get/become lost
16 take
B
1 locations　2 stands for　3 symbols　4 route
5 instructions　6 Turn　7 North　8 following
C
1 getting lost　2 taking　3 located　4 stands for
D
1 map　2 route　3 symbol　4 map key
5 intersection　6 directions

E 何謂地圖？
　　地圖是指不同地方的製圖，能夠呈現出一個地方的樣貌。有些地圖涵蓋了廣大範圍，如整個國家。有些地圖則以小區域呈現，像是城市或鄰近地區。
　　地圖可以呈現出許多事物。大地圖上有土地和水，這些地圖中有國家、海洋，甚至是大陸。人們利用這些地圖尋找國家和城市。小地圖則可能呈現出一座城市或地區，圖中有許多細節，像是獨立的建築物和街道。人們會利用這些地圖尋找方位。
* area 地區；區域　**details** 細節；詳情
individual 單獨的；個別的

填空
1 地圖呈現出一個地方的樣貌。(Maps)
2 地圖可以呈現出小區域，像是城市或鄰近地區。(cities)
3 大地圖上有國家、海洋和大陸。(seas)
4 小地圖上有獨立的建築物和街道。(buildings)

09 Unit ● Our Earth and Its Resources (p. 46)

A
1 natural resources　2 extinct　3 recycling bin
4 environment　5 responsibility　6 pollution
7 dirty　8 trash can　9 endangered
10 conservation　11 care about　12 recycle
13 reuse　14 save　15 waste
16 take care of / care for
B
1 natural resources　2 endangered
3 recycling bin　4 pollution　5 environment
6 Extinct　7 responsibility　8 Conservation
C
1 (b)　2 (a)　3 (c)
D
1 glass→④　2 paper→①　3 cans→②
4 plastic→③

世界上有許多動物。有些種類的動物數量很多，而有些種類則為數不多。這些動物瀕臨絕種，我們要是再不去注意，牠們很可能會全數死亡，並且絕種。在中國，熊貓就快要絕種。在海裡，藍鯨瀕臨絕種。在非洲，獅子、老虎和大象全都將要滅絕。還有許多其他瀕臨絕種的動物。什麼是人類可以做的呢？人們可以停止獵殺牠們，還可以把棲息地留給動物們。然後，也許有一天，牠們就不會絕種了。

*species 種類 set aside 留出；撥出

以下何者為「是」？請在空格中填入「T」或「F」。
1 所有的動物都瀕臨絕種。(F)
2 有些動物很可能全數死亡，並且絕種。(T)
3 熊貓並沒有瀕臨絕種。(F)
4 人們應該停止獵殺瀕臨絕種的動物。(T)

Unit 10 ● Native Americans and Europeans in the New World (p. 50)

A

1 Native American 2 tribe 3 New World
4 voyage 5 explorer 6 treasure 7 freedom
8 colony 9 *Mayflower* 10 discover
11 explore 12 land 13 colonize 14 settle in
15 Pilgrim 16 Puritan

B

1 Native Americans 2 *Mayflower* 3 explorer
4 voyage 5 treasure 6 New World 7 tribes
8 different

C

1 Pilgrims 2 Spanish 3 Puritans 4 colonized

D

1 Native American 2 *Mayflower*
3 the New World 4 Pilgrims
5 colony 6 Inca

E   在新世界的西班牙人

哥倫布在 1492 年發現了新世界。從那時候起，許多歐洲人便開始造訪這塊土地。大部分早期的探險家都來自西班牙。因為西班牙人想要變得更富裕，所以他們都在尋找黃金和銀。他們對待當地人通常都非常殘忍。

他們和當地人發生了衝突，西班牙人為此殺害了許多當地人。他們打敗了阿茲特克人，也擊敗了印加人，讓許多當地人成為他們的奴隸。他們完全沒有興趣和他們做朋友，他們只想要得到寶藏。

*cruel 殘忍的；殘酷的 defeat 戰勝；擊敗
Aztecs 阿茲特克人 Incas 印加人 slave 奴隸

閱讀並且回答下列問題。
1 誰發現了新世界？(Christopher Columbus)
2 西班牙探險家想要什麼？(gold and silver)
3 西班牙人打敗了哪些美國印地安人？
 (the Aztecs and Incas)
4 西班牙人對那些戰敗的美國印地安人做了什麼？
 (They made them slaves.)

Review Test 2

A

1 river 2 lake 3 Pacific Ocean 4 peninsula
5 map 6 symbol 7 map key
8 natural resources 9 extinct
10 Native American 11 be surrounded by
12 be made up of 13 be next to 14 be located/
situated in 15 mean 16 recycle 17 preserve
18 discover 19 explore 20 land

B

1 (a) 2 (b) 3 (a) 4 (c)

C

1 ocean 2 Asia 3 locations 4 Native Americans

Unit 11 ● Seasons and Weather (p. 56)

A

1 season 2 spring 3 summer 4 fall 5 winter
6 weather 7 temperature 8 blow 9 increase
10 decrease 11 rain 12 snow 13 tornado
14 lightning 15 thunder 16 storm

B

1 spring 2 temperature 3 season 4 fall
5 rainy 6 snowy 7 summer 8 winter

C

1 weather 2 gets colder 3 increases 4 snows

D

1 rainy 2 snowy 3 sunny 4 lightning
5 thunder 6 temperature

E   季節和氣候

一年有四季，分別是春天、夏天、秋天和冬天。人們有時候會用 autumn 取代 fall 的說法。每個季節的天氣都不相同。春天的氣溫變得暖和，常常都是下雨天。一切事物都恢復了生命力，花兒開始綻放，樹葉也開始茂盛起來。在夏天，天氣通常都很晴朗炎熱。到了秋天，氣溫開始下降，天氣變得涼爽，樹葉的顏色也開始改變。冬天是最寒冷的季節，通常都會下雪。

以下何者為「是」？請在空格中填入「T」或「F」。
1 fall 的另外一種說法為 autumn。(T)
2 花兒在夏天開始綻放。(F)
3 秋天的天氣比夏天更為炎熱。(F)
4 冬天可能會下雪。(T)

Unit 12 • The Parts of a Plant (p. 60)

A

1 plant   2 leaf   3 stem   4 root   5 flower   6 soil
7 nutrient   8 plant   9 water   10 bloom
11 blossom   12 grow   13 produce   14 absorb
15 branch   16 fruit

B

1 Plants   2 flower   3 Stems   4 Leaves
5 Nutrients   6 blooming   7 fruits   8 sow

C

1 (a)   2 (b)   3 (b)

D

1 Leaves   2 Stems   3 Roots   4 Flowers
5 Trunks   6 Good soil

E 如何種植物

我們在花園裡種一些植物吧。首先，我們需要一些種子。我們必須把種子種在土裡，然後澆水。經過幾天或幾個星期後，植物會開始長出地面。它們一開始長得很渺小，但會變得一天比一天還高大。

現在，植物需要充足的陽光、水分和養分才能夠茁壯。莖會慢慢地越長越高，而植物也會開始長出枝葉。有的還會開花，而這些花之後會變成我們所吃的果實。其中一部分的花會產生種子，之後又長成新的植物。

以下何者為「是」？請在空格中填入「T」或「F」。
1 植物是由種子所生長而成的。(T)
2 種子不需要水分。(F)
3 植物只需要水分和養分。(F)
4 花之後通常會結成果實。(T)

Unit 13 • Homes for Living Things (p. 64)

A

1 habitat   2 living thing   3 desert   4 forest
5 underground   6 grassland   7 environment
8 rainforest   9 life cycle   10 survive   11 stay alive
12 adapt   13 change   14 die out   15 moist
16 live in

B

1 living things   2 habitat   3 life cycle   4 forest
5 environment   6 desert   7 underground
8 live in

C

1 (c)   2 (b)   3 (b)

D

1 desert habitat   2 forest habitat
3 underground habitat   4 water habitat
5 grasslands habitat   6 rainforest habitat

E 居住地

動物的棲息地非常重要，那裡有動物生存所需的條件。大部分的動物都無法居住在其棲息地之外的地方。魚兒住在水中，而無法在沙漠中生存。鹿居住在森林裡，不能在叢林裡生存。

是什麼讓棲息地變得如此獨特呢？有許多原因，其中有兩項最為重要，也就是氣候和氣溫。這兩項條件幫助特定的植物生存。許多動物都會把這些植物當作食物和棲身之處。少了它們，動物就無法在那些地方存活。

以下何者為「是」？請在空格中填入「T」或「F」。
1 棲息地對動物來說並不重要。(F)
2 鹿可以在叢林中生存。(F)
3 一個棲息地的氣候非常重要。(T)
4 動物會把植物當成棲身之處。(T)

Unit 14 • Oceans and Undersea Life (p. 68)

A

1 ocean   2 tide   3 shore   4 ocean current
5 plankton   6 salt water   7 fresh water
8 undersea   9 rise   10 fall   11 water level
12 dolphin   13 tuna   14 trench   15 water pollution
16 coral reef

B

1 Tides   2 oceans   3 plankton   4 salt water
5 water level   6 Water pollution   7 undersea
8 Coral reefs

C

1 rises   2 drops   3 shore   4 carry

D

1 fresh water   2 trench   3 salt water
4 shore

E 捕魚和捕魚過度

海洋為許多植物和動物提供了不同的棲息地，幫助地球保持健康。因此，我們必須小心避免對海洋造成傷害。

世界上有很多人喜歡吃海產，我們所吃的海產都是漁夫從海裡捕撈的，其中包括水生有殼動物和魚類。水生有殼動物是指蝦子、蛤蜊、螃蟹和龍蝦。由於人們吃很多海產，所以也有很多漁夫。不幸的是，近年來漁夫捕捉過量的魚類，造成魚兒的數目減少。許多捕魚區的面積變得越來越小。漁夫必須要停止大量捕捉魚類，他們必須給魚兒們繁殖的時間。

* overfishing（魚的）過度捕撈   **shellfish** 水生有殼動物
fishing ground 捕魚區

閱讀並且回答下列問題。
1 海洋為地球帶來什麼樣的幫助？(stay healthy)
2 漁夫捕捉的是什麼？(fish and shellfish)
3 現今的漁夫捕捉了多少魚？(too many)
4 捕魚區變得如何了？(They are getting smaller.)

A

1 bone 2 skeleton 3 muscle 4 heart 5 blood
6 brain 7 nerve 8 germ 9 digest 10 saliva
11 pump 12 beat 13 break down 14 digestive
system 15 nervous system 16 muscular system

B

1 bones 2 skeleton 3 nervous system
4 digests 5 germs 6 Muscles 7 heart
8 circulates

C

1 pumps 2 send 3 break down 4 carries

D

1 sight 2 hearing 3 smell 4 taste 5 touch
6 heart

E 保持健康

　　人體就像是機器，許多部位都有助於身體維持運作。如果這些部位正常運轉，這個人就很健康。但人類的身體有時也會故障，而這個人也就生病了。

　　細菌常常會使人生病。當細菌攻擊人體時，身體必須反擊回去。人體有時能夠獨自對抗細菌，但有時可能會需要藉由醫生所開的藥物以恢復健康。幸虧許多藥物都能夠殺死細菌，並且幫助身體再度恢復健康。

* **break down** 失敗；故障　**get sick** 生病　**attack** 攻擊
　fight back 反擊　**defeat** 擊敗　**medicine** 藥物

填空

1 身體就像是機器。(machine)
2 人體有時候也會故障。(breaks)
3 細菌有時會使人生病。(Germs)
4 醫生所開的藥能使人們恢復健康。(medicine)

Review Test 3

A

1 plant 2 leaf 3 stem 4 root 5 season
6 weather 7 habitat 8 living thing 9 skeleton
10 muscle 11 grow 12 rain 13 snow 14 fall
15 water level 16 whale 17 taste 18 live in
19 digest 20 nervous system

B

1 (a) 2 (b) 3 (c) 4 (b)

C

1 Stems 2 season 3 Tides 4 habitat

A

1 solid 2 liquid 3 gas 4 matter 5 form
6 state 7 heat 8 cool 9 change into 10 boil
11 touch 12 feel 13 become 14 freeze
15 melt 16 air

B

1 liquid 2 states 3 gas 4 boil 5 melt
6 change 7 Solids 8 touch

C

1 freeze 2 solid 3 heat 4 cool

D

1 a liquid 2 a gas 3 a gas 4 a solid 5 a liquid
6 a solid

E 水會如何變化？

　　水有三種狀態：固體、液體或氣體。為何它會改變呢？因為「溫度」。水的正常狀態為液體，但有時也會變成固體。為什麼呢？因為過冷。當熱被帶走時，水會結冰。固態的水稱為冰。還有，水有時也會變氣體。為什麼呢？因為過熱。當溫度夠高的時候，水會沸騰，然後會變成蒸氣，而這種蒸氣就是氣體。當水變成氣體時，稱為水蒸氣。

* **normal** 正常的；標準的　**take away** 帶走；拿走
　steam 蒸氣　**water vapor** 水蒸氣

填空

1 水可以是固體、液體或氣體。(liquid)
2 水的正常狀態為液體。(state)
3 固態的水稱為冰。(ice)
4 溫度變高時，水會沸騰。(boils)

A

1 measure 2 inch 3 length 4 distance
5 height 6 temperature 7 thermometer
8 weight 9 pound 10 foot 11 take 12 fill
13 pour 14 measure height 15 measure length
16 measure the amount

B

1 measure 2 weight 3 foot 4 height
5 temperature 6 thermometer 7 Fill
8 calculated

C

1 meters 2 inches 3 pounds 4 take

D

1 height 2 length 3 weight 4 temperature

E 測量食物

　　來做一些餅乾吧。我們備齊了所有的材料。現在，在開始製作前，我們必須先測量。

　　首先，我們需要一杯奶油。然後我們需要 $\frac{3}{4}$ 杯的白糖，還有等量的紅糖，以及 $2\frac{1}{4}$ 杯的麵粉。我們還需要 $1\frac{1}{2}$

茶匙的香草精、1 茶匙的蘇打粉，和 $\frac{1}{2}$ 茶匙的鹽。我們同時也需要量出 $1\frac{1}{2}$ 杯的巧克力碎片。最後，我們需要 2 顆雞蛋。現在，我們已經測量出所有的材料了。開始製作吧。
* **ingredient** 原料　**extract** 提取物；精；汁

閱讀並且回答下列問題。
1 此人在製作什麼東西？(cookies)
2 需要多少的紅糖？($\frac{3}{4}$cup)
3 需要多少的巧克力碎片？($1\frac{1}{2}$cups)
4 需要幾顆雞蛋？(2)

18 ● Electricity (p. 86)

A
1 electricity　2 energy　3 lightning　4 wire
5 battery　6 switch　7 lightbulb　8 experiment
9 current　10 power company　11 turn on
12 turn off　13 flow　14 move　15 electric power
16 cell phone battery
B
1 current　2 battery　3 switch　4 energy
5 Electricity　6 lightning bolt　7 experiment
8 lightbulb
C
1 flow　2 plug　3 electrical appliances
4 electricity
D
1 outlet　2 battery　3 plug　4 switch
5 lightbulb　6 lightning
E　班哲明‧富蘭克林
　　班哲明‧富蘭克林是一位偉大的美國科學家，他活在 200 多年前。他對閃電非常好奇。他認為那是電，但他並不確定。因此，他決定做一項實驗。
　　富蘭克林在風箏上綁了一支金屬製的鑰匙，然後等著暴風雨的來臨。他在暴風雨中放風箏，而閃電打中了那個地方。閃電產生的電荷擊中了鑰匙。當富蘭克林觸摸鑰匙時，他休克了。他證實了閃電是電的一種！
* **metal** 金屬；金屬製品　**kite** 風箏　**strike** 擊；打
　electric charge 電荷　**get shocked** 休克

填空
1 班哲明‧富蘭克林是一位科學家。(scientist)
2 富蘭克林相信閃電是電。(lightning)
3 富蘭克林在暴風雨中放風箏。(kite)
4 當富蘭克林觸摸鑰匙時，他休克了。(key)

19 ● Our Solar System (p. 90)

A
1 Mercury　2 Venus　3 Earth　4 Mars　5 Jupiter
6 Saturn　7 Uranus　8 Neptune　9 go around
10 orbit　11 planet　12 comet　13 satellite
14 space shuttle　15 space station　16 go down
B
1 goes down　2 star　3 Venus　4 Pluto　5 Saturn
6 Uranus　7 Neptune　8 moon
C
1 goes around　2 sets　3 planets　4 satellite
D
1 orbit　2 rise　3 set　4 Mars　5 Saturn
6 Jupiter
E　冥王星是行星嗎？
　　太陽系是指太陽和圍繞著太陽運轉的行星，共有八大行星。與太陽的距離從近到遠依序為：水星、金星、地球、火星、木星、土星、天王星和海王星。科學家曾認為冥王星是太陽系中的第九大行星，但他們現在改變了看法。他們認為冥王星是顆小行星。外太陽系有許多類似冥王星的物體，而科學家並不認為它們是行星。因此，他們不再把冥王星當作是行星。
* **consider** 認為　**minor planet** 小行星
　outer solar system 外太陽系

以下何者為「是」？請在空格中填入「T」或「F」。
1 太陽系中共有九大行星。(F)
2 土星是距離太陽第五個位置的行星。(F)
3 冥王星被認為是太陽系中的第九大行星。(F)
4 外太陽系有許多類似冥王星的物體。(T)

20 ● Inside the earth (p. 94)

A
1 surface　2 layer　3 core　4 crust　5 mantle
6 volcano　7 lava　8 hot spring　9 mineral
10 continent　11 ocean　12 pole　13 erupt
14 spew　15 melt　16 be covered with
B
1 surface　2 layers　3 volcano　4 melt
5 spewed　6 hot springs　7 erupt　8 poles
C
1 Lava　2 continents　3 Pacific　4 minerals
D
1 surface　2 layers　3 crust　4 mantle　5 core
6 lava

地球是一顆巨大的行星，總共分為三部分：地殼、地幔和核心，而每個部分都不相同。

地殼是地球的最外層，也就是地球的表面。海洋、河流、山、沙漠和森林等所有在地球表面的東西都是地殼的一部分。地殼下有一層高溫、熔化的厚岩石，稱為地幔。地幔佔了最大的比例，溫度非常的高。地球最內部的部分稱為核心，其中有些部分是固態，而有些是液態。

* **outermost** 最外邊的　**extremely** 非常；極其
innermost 最內部的

閱讀並且回答下列問題。
1 地球共有幾個部分？(three)
2 地球的表面稱為什麼？(the crust)
3 佔地球最大比例的是哪個部分？(the mantle)
4 地球的最內部稱為什麼？(the core)

Review Test 4

A
1 solid　2 liquid　3 gas　4 measure　5 length
6 electricity　7 energy　8 Mercury　9 Venus
10 surface　11 change into　12 measure height
13 measure length　14 turn on　15 flow　16 go
around　17 planet　18 crust　19 mantle
20 core

B
1 (a)　2 (b)　3 (b)　4 (c)

C
1 states　2 weight　3 Saturn　4 layers

Unit 21 ● Shapes (p. 100)

A
1 rectangle　2 square　3 triangle　4 circle
5 oval　6 cube　7 pentagon　8 hexagon
9 side　10 edge　11 flat shape　12 solid shape
13 cylinder　14 sphere　15 sort　16 resemble

B
1 sides　2 edges　3 solid shapes　4 differs
5 circle　6 similar to　7 globe　8 classify

C
1 oval　2 square　3 cube　4 flat shapes

D
1 triangle　2 flat shapes　3 solid shapes
4 sphere　5 resemble　6 classify

E 五種簡單的形狀

基本形狀有五種：正方形、長方形、三角形、圓形和橢圓形。還有許多其他的形狀，但都和這五種基本形狀相似。

每個物體都有一定的形狀。例如，一個盒子可能看起來像正方形或長方形。立體的物體也一樣。一片披薩可能會像三角形；足球和棒球都是圓形的；而雞蛋是橢圓形的。還有其他更多複雜的形狀。一座山可能像是一座金字塔；而漏斗看起來像是圓錐體。

* **object** 物體　**complicated** 複雜的

以下何者為「是」？請在空格中填入「T」或「F」。
1 立方體是五種基本形狀之一。(F)
2 有些盒子看起來像圓形。(F)
3 雞蛋的形狀像橢圓形。(T)
4 有些山看起來像金字塔。(T)

Unit 22 ● Numbers and Counting (p. 104)

A
1 zero　2 count　3 compare　4 greater than
5 less than　6 equal to　7 first　8 second
9 order　10 dozen　11 count by tens
12 count forward　13 count backward
14 place value　15 digit　16 ordinal numbers

B
1 Count　2 tens　3 Compare　4 greater
5 less than　6 equal to　7 digits　8 place value

C
1 after　2 backward　3 9　4 equal to

D
1 greater than　2 less than　3 equal to　4 zero
5 dozen　6 digits

E 比大和比小

所有的數字都有一定的數值，因此有些數字會比其他數字大，而有些數字會比其他數字小。

在後面的數字會比前面的數字大。舉例來說，6 在 5 的後面，所以我們會說：「6 比 5 大」。在數學的術語中，我們會寫成：「6 > 5」。在前面的數字會比後面的數字小。舉例來說 2 在 3 的前面，所以我們會說：「2 比 3 小」。在數學的術語中，我們會寫成：「2 < 3」。

填空
1 有些數字會比其他數字大。(than)
2 6 在 5 的後面。(after)
3 5 比 4 大。(greater)
4 2 比 3 小。(less)

Unit ● Addition and Subtraction (p. 108)

A
1 addition　2 subtraction　3 add　4 subtract
5 sum　6 difference　7 solve　8 problem
9 is　10 is equal to　11 equals　12 take away
13 find　14 an equal sign　15 a minus sign
16 a plus sign

B
1 equals　2 Find　3 Solve　4 add　5 Take away
6 problem　7 Addition　8 minus sign

C
1 minus　2 plus　3 difference　4 sum

D
1 + (a plus sign)　2 − (a minus sign)
3 = (an equal sign)　4 > (greater than)
5 < (less than)　6 = (an equal sign)

E 加法和減法
　　加法就是把兩個或兩個以上的數字相加。在做加法的時候，所得到的答案稱為「總和」。舉例來說，5＋2 的總和為 7。減法就是把一個數字減去另一個數字。假設你有 5 顆蘋果，你拿了 2 顆給你的弟弟。還剩下幾顆？原本有 5 顆，但你拿走了 2 顆，所以現在有 3 顆。 5-2=3。剩下的數字稱為差額。所以 5-2 的差額為 3。

以下何者為非？(1)
1 把兩個數字相加稱為減法。
2 5 加上 2 的總和為 7。
3 5 減去 2 等於 3。
4 5-2 的差額為 3。

24 **Unit ● Counting Money (p. 112)**

A
1 money　2 coin　3 bill　4 one cent　5 nickel
6 dime　7 quarter　8 half-dollar　9 penny
10 dollar　11 amount　12 one-dollar bill
13 ten-dollar bill　14 exchange　15 combine
16 be worth

B
1 Money　2 amount　3 quarter　4 Exchange
5 value　6 is worth　7 pennies　8 Combine

C
1 dime　2 half-dollar　3 nickel　4 quarter

D
1 nickel　2 dime　3 quarter　4 half-dollar
5 penny　6 dollar

E 換零錢
　　人們用錢來購買許多不同的物品和服務。紙鈔和硬幣都屬於錢，所有的紙鈔和硬幣價值都不相同。學著辨別硬幣，就能夠知道其價值。假設你在商店買糖果，花了 75 分錢，因此你可以拿一元給店員。一元值 100 分錢。你會

找回多少零錢呢？25 分錢。你會拿到一個 25 分硬幣，但也許你並不想要 25 分硬幣。因此，告訴店員：「請給我兩個十分錢和一個五分錢。」這就是換零錢的方式。
＊**change** 交換；改變　**recognize** 辨別　**cost** 花費

閱讀並且回答下列問題。
1 人們會用錢來買什麼東西？(goods and services)
2 每個硬幣都有什麼？(its own value)
3 一個四分之一元價值多少？(twenty-five cents)
4 哪些硬幣的價值相加等於一個 25 分硬幣？
　(2 dimes and 1 nickel)

Review Test 5

A
1 rectangle　2 square　3 triangle　4 circle
5 addition　6 subtraction　7 sum　8 money
9 amount　10 dozen　11 add　12 subtract
13 coin　14 bill　15 exchange　16 be worth
17 greater than　18 less than　19 equals　20 order

B
1 (a)　2 (b)　3 (a)

C
1 sides　2 edges　3 Solve　4 add　5 value
6 worth

25 **Unit ● Read and Write (p. 118)**

A
1 uppercase/capital letter　2 lowercase/small letter
3 rule　4 grammar　5 sentence　6 punctuation
7 alphabet　8 pronounce　9 letter　10 sound
11 word　12 spelling　13 handwriting　14 period
15 comma　16 communicate with

B
1 pronounce　2 singular　3 uppercase letter
4 Small letters　5 handwriting
6 Punctuation marks　7 sound
8 communicate with

C
1 rules　2 plural　3 capital　4 words

D
1 sentence　2 capital letter　3 small letter
4 punctuation

❶ 2017 年 8 月 31 日

親愛的約翰：❷

我的名字叫作莎拉。❸

我住在韓國首爾。你住在哪裡呢？❹

我就讀於中央國小。❺

我喜歡騎腳踏車。

請回信給我，並且告訴我關於你的事情。

真摯地 ❻

莎拉

❶ 日期：先在最上方寫上日期。月份的字首要大寫。
❷ 問候：以 Dear 作為問候的開頭。要用大寫字母 D。
❸ 大寫：句首的字母要大寫。
❹ 問句：問句句末要使用問號。
❺ 名字：人名、地名或特定事物的名稱字首要大寫。
❻ 結尾：信末以結尾辭和名字作結。
　　　結尾辭字首要大寫，後面要使用逗號。
　　　別忘了你的名字字首也要用大寫。

填空
1 信件最上方要有日期。(date)
2 問句句末要使用問號。(questions)
3 人名、地名或特定事物的名稱字首要大寫。(capital)
4 結尾辭後面要有逗號。(comma)

Unit 26 ● Types of Writing (p. 122)

A
1 poem　2 novel　3 drama　4 fairy tale　5 fable
6 literature　7 saying, proverb　8 character
9 rhyme　10 folk tale　11 memorize　12 remember
13 choose　14 story　15 lesson　16 nonfiction

B
1 drama　2 folk tale　3 fairy tale　4 Fiction
5 Fables　6 moral　7 rhyme　8 characters

C
1 (b)　2 (a)　3 (b)

D
1 character　2 fiction　3 fable　4 poem
5 saying, proverb　6 pick, select

E　伊索寓言
　　伊索是古希臘的一位奴隸，他活在二千多年前。他因講述他所蒐集的故事而聞名，也就是現在的《伊索寓言》。
　　《伊索寓言》有很多簡短的故事，通常以動物為主角。透過關於動物的故事，伊索教導我們人類該有何種行為舉止。在寓言的結尾，伊索通常會讓我們上了一課，而這一課就是指故事的寓意。他有許多故事至今仍非常有名。《龜兔賽跑》非常受歡迎，《螞蟻與蚱蜢》也是，而《獅子與老鼠》和《狐狸與葡萄》也很有名。

以下何者為「是」？請在空格中填入「T」或「F」。
1 伊索是古希臘的國王。(F)
2 《伊索寓言》是長篇故事。(F)
3 《伊索寓言》中的主角通常都是動物。(T)
4 《螞蟻與老鼠》是《伊索寓言》中有名的故事。(F)

Unit 27 ● A World of Lines and Colors (p. 126)

A
1 shape　2 texture　3 painting　4 sculpture
5 portrait　6 mural　7 statue　8 drawing
9 paint　10 create　11 mix colors　12 straight line
13 curved line　14 sculptor　15 painter　16 artist

B
1 primary colors　2 painted　3 make colors
4 painter　5 sculptor　6 Statue　7 artist
8 making

C
1 paintings　2 mix colors　3 shapes　4 lines

D
1 mix colors　2 green　3 red, yellow, and blue
4 portrait　5 mural　6 drawing

E　三原色和第二次色
　　基本顏色有三種，分別是紅色、黃色和藍色，我們稱之為三原色。把這些顏色混合在一起，你就可以調出其他顏色。例如，把紅色和黃色混合就能夠調配出橘色。把黃色和藍色混合就能夠變成綠色。還有，混合紅色和藍色就會調出紫色或紫羅蘭色。這些顏色我們稱為第二次色。
　　當然，還有許多其他的顏色。你可以把紅色、黃色和藍色混合調出黑色，也可以把三原色和第二次色混合變成其他顏色。

*primary 基本的；主要的　secondary 第二的　combine 使結合

填空
1 紅色、黃色和藍色是三原色。(yellow)
2 綠色、橘色和紫色是第二次色。(secondary)
3 把紅色和藍色混合會變成紫色。(purple or violet)
4 黑色是由紅色、黃色和藍色組合而成的。(Black)

A

1 still life 2 landscape 3 brushstroke 4 trace
5 sculpt 6 arrange 7 look at 8 sketch
9 touch 10 tone 11 object 12 watercolor
13 oils 14 paints 15 easel 16 canvas

B

1 brushstrokes 2 made 3 drawn 4 arrange
5 Oils 6 tones 7 tracing paper 8 touch

C

1 Watercolor pictures 2 sculpt 3 canvas

D

1 landscape 2 still life 3 brush 4 crayon
5 sketch 6 observe

E 名畫家

　畫廊展示了許多畫家的作品。在這麼多畫家之中，其中有些非常有名。藝術家繪製了許多不同類型的畫，而每幅畫都有難以言喻的美。

　畢卡索是一位有名的現代畫家，而馬奈、莫內、塞尚和梵谷是 100 多年前的畫家。李奧那多・達文西也非常有名，他畫了一幅全世界最有名的畫：《蒙娜麗莎》。林布蘭也是很久以前的畫家，還有米開朗基羅，他是約 500 年前的畫家。

* art gallery 畫廊　**display** 展示
in one's own way 難以言喻地

閱讀並且回答下列問題。
1 哪裡能夠觀賞畫家的作品？(at an art gallery)
2 有名的現代畫家叫作什麼名字？(Picasso)
3《蒙娜麗莎》是誰畫的？(Leonardo da Vinci)
4 米開朗基羅是多久以前的畫家？(around 500 years ago)

A

1 (musical) instrument 2 orchestra 3 composer
4 conductor 5 musician 6 play, perform
7 compose, write 8 read music, read musical
notes 9 play a musical instrument 10 piano solo
11 piano duet 12 pianist 13 guitarist 14 violinist
15 drummer 16 trumpeter

B

1 orchestra 2 read music 3 play 4 conduct
5 write 6 composers 7 musical instruments
8 singers

C

1 keyboards 2 violin 3 trumpet 4 flute

D

1 conductor 2 composer 3 musician
4 play 5 compose 6 orchestra

E 音樂家和樂器

　樂器有許多種類。由於樂器能夠製造出不同的聲音，所以音樂分為許多種。搖滾音樂家通常會運用吉他和鼓；爵士樂需要鋼琴和薩克斯風；古典音樂則運用了許多不同種類的樂器。

　人們通常會一起演奏兩種以上的樂器，組成一支樂團或管弦樂隊，不過，這些音樂家必須同時間演奏。他們大多數都會讀譜，這樣他們才知道要演奏哪個音符。如果他們同時都能夠演奏得很好，就可以創造出和諧的音樂。

* harmonious 和諧的；協調的

以下何者為「是」？請在空格中填入「T」或「F」。
1 爵士音樂家常彈奏鋼琴。(T)
2 鼓在搖滾樂中相當普遍。(T)
3 一支樂團只需要一項樂器。(F)
4 音樂家讀譜是為了學習如何演奏樂器。(F)

A

1 melody 2 words 3 tune 4 harmony
5 rhythm 6 beat 7 opera 8 ballet 9 audience
10 whole note 11 half note 12 read music
13 performer 14 hum 15 keep time
16 play music

B

1 rhythm 2 harmony 3 make 4 words
5 keep time 6 audience

C

1 (b) 2 (a) 3 (b) 4 (c)

D

1 singer 2 performer 3 audience 4 note
5 opera 6 ballet

E 受歡迎的兒歌

　一首歌為何會受到歡迎呢？這其中有許多原因。最簡單的歌曲往往會最受歡迎，因為簡單的歌詞容易使人記住。或者是因為容易演奏或記住的旋律，讓人們可以經常哼出或用口哨吹出音樂。

　有些歌曲相當受到年輕人喜愛，〈Bingo〉是其中一首歌曲，還有〈王老先生有塊地〉、〈小星星〉和西班牙文歌曲〈蟑螂〉。人們為什麼喜歡這些歌曲呢？因為歌詞常常重複、押韻，以及曲調都很動聽且容易記住。

* factor 因素　**involved** 有關的　**rhyme** 押韻
catchy 動聽且容易記住的

填空
1 簡單的歌曲往往都很受歡迎。(simple)
2 有些人喜歡哼或用口哨吹出音樂。(hum)
3〈小星星〉是一首廣受年輕人喜愛的歌曲。(Star)
4 受歡迎的歌曲往往都有動聽且容易記住的曲調。(catchy)

A

1 grammar 2 sentence 3 painting 4 sculpture
5 (musical) instrument 6 orchestra 7 composer
8 play, perform 9 compose, write
10 read music, read musical notes
11 paint 12 portrait 13 audience
14 classical music 15 keep time 16 play music
17 memorize 18 choose
19 read aloud / read out loud 20 fiction

B

1 (b) 2 (a) 3 (b) 4 (a)

C

1 drama 2 drawn 3 orchestra 4 rhythm